INFERNO!

Tom and Rob followed Captain Invisible into the jewelry store. Tom removed a flashlight from his pocket and turned it on the costumed thief. "Now, Rob!" Rob and Tom started toward the masked hoodlum.

But as Tom went to take another step, he found himself looking at the floor. Rob had knocked him down—just a microsecond before a bullet whizzed through the space where Tom had been standing.

Tom crouched and counted. Five, six, seven shots. And then a distinct click. "That's it, Rob. He's out of ammo. Charge him!"

Before Rob could act, Captain Invisible took an object from a belt around his waist and threw it at Tom with all his might.

With electronic speed, Rob caught the missile in midair. The firebomb exploded on contact and burst into flames. Within moments, Tom was surrounded by a raging inferno—and there was no way out.

Books in the Tom Swift® Series

Available from ARCHWAY Paperbacks

TOM SWIFT

FIRE BIKER

VICTOR APPLETON

AN ARCHWAY PAPERBACK
Published by POCKET BOOKS
New York   London   Toronto   Sydney   Tokyo   Singapore

AN ARCHWAY PAPERBACK *Original*

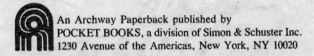

An Archway Paperback published by
POCKET BOOKS, a division of Simon & Schuster Inc.
1230 Avenue of the Americas, New York, NY 10020

Copyright © 1992 by Simon & Schuster Inc.

Produced by Byron Preiss Visual Publications, Inc.

ISBN: 0-671-75652-4

First Archway Paperback printing June 1992

10 9 8 7 6 5 4 3 2 1

TOM SWIFT, AN ARCHWAY PAPERBACK and colophon are registered trademarks of Simon & Schuster Inc.

Cover art by Romas Kukalis

Printed in the U.S.A.

IL 6+

FIRE BIKER

1

YAAHOOO!" TOM SWIFT WHOOPED AS HE soared over the huge complex that was Swift Enterprises. He swooped down and stopped dead in the air outside the window of his father's office, at the corner of the fourth floor of the administration building.

Behind the glass, Thomas Swift, Sr., was pleased. "Congratulations, son," he said into his throat mike. "You've designed a rather nice machine there."

Tom smiled, knowing his father's comment was an intentional understatement. Tom was riding what looked like a cross between a heavy motorcycle and a Harrier jump-jet, although it owed nothing to either.

On either side of the central frame, whose tandem, retractable wheels gave it only the vaguest resemblance to a motorcycle, were rotatable turbofan lifters. These could propel the contraption forward at half the speed of sound, or lift it vertically to twenty-five thousand feet or more. The jet cycle's computerized fly-by-wire control system was so simple to operate, Tom had needed only a few ground-tethered tests before he unleashed its full power and put on the demonstration for his father.

As Tom hovered, a big, broad-shouldered guy watched the show from the parking lot below. He couldn't resist adding his own comment. "It's also got nice colors," he radioed.

That, too, was an understatement. Because Rick Cantwell had helped Tom with the tests, Tom had made the mistake of allowing his friend to select the color scheme. Now scarlet and yellow flames wrapped the big turbo-lifter casings in fluorescent glory.

"At least I won't have to worry about collisions with birds," Tom had commented when he had seen the result of Rick's artistry the day before. "One look, and the shock will cause them to fall out of the sky!"

"Plucked and cooked," Tom's friend Mandy Coster had added with a wink at Sandra, Tom's sister.

Mr. Swift made no comment about the jet cycle's vivid color scheme. He merely said, "Better bring it in, Tom. Don't forget you still have performance checks to run."

Tom played with the controls, and the jet cycle weaved side to side and up and down—literally a dance. "What checks, Dad?" he demanded. "'You can see for yourself. The bike performs perfectly."

Rick cut in. "Hey, Tom, remember Sandra? Your sister? I don't know what it's about, but she told me she'd be mad enough to use your head for softball practice if you didn't meet her as promised at ten o'clock!"

"Oh, no! I forgot." Tom glanced at the heads-up time display in his helmet: 10:08. He acknowledged Rick with a wave and sent the jet cycle zooming over the office complex of Swift Enterprises and on toward the experimental labs.

"I am in major trouble," he groaned. "Rick, walk over to the test facility marked Building Twenty-three. I'll leave the jet cycle outside. Take it back to the garage, break it down, and run tolerance and quality checks on *everything*. If Sandra doesn't kill me, I'll meet you there around two o'clock.''

But Sandra was in a good mood when Tom sheepishly turned up at the Volatiles Test facility twenty minutes late. ''What did Dad think of the bike?'' she asked.

Tom was already pulling on the garment she had been checking when he arrived. ''The word he used was 'nice,' '' he replied with a grin.

''Oh well, we both know Dad's not the jump-up-and-down type. What about Rick? He likes the bike, doesn't he?''

''He'd better,'' Tom joked. ''After all, he painted it!''

Having already been told at least a dozen times what her brother thought of the jet cycle's eye-catching color scheme, Sandra laughed as she busied herself checking various seals and fastenings on the garment. ''How does that feel?'' she asked.

''Just a minute.'' Tom flexed his knees and twisted his body. The shimmering, flexible suit that covered him from neck to toe was astonishingly comfortable, and he found he could move just as easily as if he were in only his regular clothing, which usually was jeans and a T-shirt.

''It feels good,'' Tom said.

''Try the hood.''

"Right." Tom reached behind his neck, flipped the suit's hood over his head, and attached it to the neck ring.

Sandra laughed. "Now you look like an alien!"

"What?" he shouted, wishing they had taken the time to install a communications link in the suit. In this instance, though, Sandra had been in a hurry.

"I said, you look weird!" his sister shouted back.

Tom did not doubt that. The big goggles that were built into the hood, and the snout that contained the breathing mask and the air cooler and filter, probably made him look like a humanoid who was descended from insects. He partly unhooked the hood and lifted it from his face. "Let's get on with the test, okay?"

"What's the matter? Got a date with Mandy?" Sandra teased.

"None of your business!" Tom retorted.

Sandra took a deep breath and expelled it. "All right. We'll proceed as planned."

She followed Tom through the automatic fire door and into the concrete vault where they were to conduct the test. As Tom carefully resealed the hood, Sandra knelt by the pile of wood, paper, oily rags, and other combustibles the two of them had collected the evening before.

"Here goes," Sandra muttered as she struck a match and lit the bottom of the pile. Almost instantly, it caught.

"Better get out of here!" Tom shouted, as flames and smoke began to fill the space with astonishing rapidity.

"Right!" Sandra waved and ran around the burning pile toward the door. But something strange was happening to her—her vision wavered and she began to stagger. The door seemed to be an enormous distance away and retreated even further as she reached desperately for it. She dropped to her knees and tried to crawl, but her muscles were like jelly and she couldn't breathe.

Must be like drowning, Sandra thought as she sank to the floor and darkness claimed her.

She did not see the door's two tons of steel and ceramic slide into its frame, nor did she hear it lock with a firm metallic click.

On the other side of the fire, Tom took several deep breaths and walked back and forth a few steps. Although he was close to the flames, he felt perfectly comfortable. He touched the control on his neck ring that activated the suit's emergency compressed air supply and immediately felt a waft of cool air on his cheeks.

He reached a gloved hand into the fire and felt no heat. He deliberately walked forward into the fire and stood with the flames leaping about him. He felt only a slight warmth around his eyes as a tiny fraction of the heat penetrated the resistant glass of the goggles.

Tom grinned. He was proud of his sister and what she had accomplished. The idea for the suit had come to Sandra when a friend of hers, a fellow student at Jefferson High, had died in a house fire. The girl's bedroom had been completely engulfed in flames, yet she had not died of burns, but of smoke inhalation. The fire fighters had been unable to get into the bedroom because their equipment could not protect them from the raging blaze and toxic smoke. The tragedy had upset Sandra so much that she promptly decided to devise a better form of fire protection.

The result was a paper-thin, mirror-surface fire suit that Sandra hoped would eventually become standard fire-fighting equipment all over the world. The secret of the suit was buckycloth, which was made from C-60—a peculiar kind of carbon with large, spherical molecules called buckminsterfullerenes, or buckyballs for short.

The suit had already successfully withstood temperatures that would melt metal, but this was the first test with a human being inside the suit. Nevertheless, Tom was serenely confident as he stomped up and down in the flames like a biblical character walking through a fiery furnace.

The fire was now burning furiously, an inferno of smoke and flame that filled an entire end of the long test vault.

Suddenly Tom was startled by an enormous *whoof,* and the vault and everything within it abruptly vanished from his view. Something in the burning material had exploded into black, impenetrable smoke. He couldn't detect even a glimmer of light, neither from the flames of the fire nor from the flameproof light fixtures that rimmed the vault. If it wasn't for the LED temperature indication inside his hood, Tom would have thought he was blind.

"Sandra?" he yelled. Then he realized there was no way his sister could hear him. At that moment she would be outside the vault, watching through the small Armorglass window so she could trigger the fire retardant sprays and then open the door when he signaled.

But how will she see my signal in this murk? Tom thought. And what was burning to make the smoke so thick, anyway? Again he regretted the lack of a communications link.

Tom began to work his way around the vault. He couldn't see a thing, so he used his hands to grope along the concrete wall toward the door, where the smoke was thinner. As well as a comm-link, Tom realized, the suit needed a miniature radar unit so its wearer could navigate through the thickest smoke. He made a mental note to work on adding such a device.

Suddenly, just as he felt the frame of the door, Tom stumbled over something. He reached down and, to his horror, discovered his sister's prone body on the floor. He shook her.

"Sandra!" Tom yelled, but she didn't stir. According to his hood indication, the temperature at this cooler end of the vault was 130 degrees Fahrenheit and rising. Tom knew his sister wasn't protected against such heat.

First he tried the door. It was closed solid and wouldn't budge.

After a moment of muscle-numbing panic, Tom swung Sandra around so that she was lying with her face close to any trickle of outside air that might be seeping under the door.

His mind racing, Tom reasoned that when Sandra had switched the fire-retardant sprays to manual control, she had forgotten to inform Megatron, the supercomputer that ran much of the electronic operations at Swift Enterprises. Megatron had detected the fire, but got a negative response in its attempt to operate the sprays and had automatically closed the door to isolate the fire. Tom knew the door would not open again until the fire was out and the room temperature was down to a normal level.

Desperate for help, Tom pressed his goggled head against the door and shouted. No response. He even banged and kicked the door, again without result.

Tom knew he and Sandra would not be in this mess if he had brought either Rob or Orb to assist. But because Tom had underestimated the potential hazards of the fire suit test, he had already assigned both robots to a detailed checkout of the jet cycle.

By now Tom was frantic. Without air, Sandra wouldn't be able to survive more than another minute or two, and he didn't have much more than that. The prototype suit's emergency air supply was good for only five minutes.

Suddenly Tom's gloved hand touched something on the wall alongside the door. Of course—the touch-key pad!

Although he couldn't see the pad in the blackness, Tom was reasonably confident he could operate the keys—if he could remember the override code that opened the door.

Mainly used by the maintenance staff, the override codes were not usually committed to memory. Instead, they were kept on a list that Tom had seen a few days earlier in the Maintenance Engineering office.

Tom willed himself to a state of calm, taking deep, even breaths. Moments later, the complete list of numbers popped into his head.

Tom's fingers moved like lightning as he tapped out the numbers. He couldn't remember which code did what, so he punched them all in as fast as he could. Finally, with his air almost gone, the vault's fire-retardant system was activated, and he and Sandra were suddenly drenched with foam.

Okay, Tom thought, the fire is out. But I still have to get Sandra out of here!

Tom began to sweat, and not from the

heat, as his fingers continued to hit key after key on the touch pad. He didn't know what else he was causing to happen in the plant, and at that moment, he didn't care.

He only knew that Sandra was gasping out her life.

SANDRA NEEDS AIR! THE THOUGHT screamed in Tom's mind. There was only one thing to do. He would remove the breathing hood from his suit and place it over Sandra's head, giving her the precious remaining minutes of oxygen. Tom started to unfasten the hood, when suddenly the smoky gloom lightened and he heard the bass rumble of the safety door sliding open.

He had done it!

Hoping he wasn't too late, Tom scooped Sandra up in his arms and ran with her toward the infirmary. She feels so light, I could carry ten of her, Tom thought as he ran down the broad corridor past the labs, past robotics, and then along the length of the administration block to the infirmary.

The startled nurse stared when she saw a shimmering, goggle-eyed monster skid to a halt and place Sandra's body on the gurney next to her desk.

Tom flipped back his hood. "Heat and smoke inhalation," he gasped. "Do something!" Then he keeled over in a dead faint.

"I am so embarrassed," Sandra Swift moaned. Her gaze shifted from her father to her brother as she lay recovering in the infirmary. "It was my mistake that nearly got us killed."

Mr. Swift patted her shoulder reassuringly. "The important thing is that you two are all right. Anyway, now that you've scared me half out of my wits, how was the test?"

Tom burped. He had just eaten a gargantuan meal—which was unusual for him—and he was still hungry. "The fire suit's perfect, Dad. I think I could have walked on the sun and felt cool!"

"It's not *that* good," Sandra said modestly.

Her father gave a sharp laugh. "Well, it did give your brother time enough to set off half the alarms in the complex and upset a lot of production schedules."

Tom blushed. "Sorry about that."

"So you should be."

"Does anyone know what caused me to pass out?" Sandra asked.

"I've thought about that," Tom said. "I think it has something to do with the satellite cannon."

Sandra was puzzled. "The what?"

Her father explained. "We're designing a supergun to replace rockets for delivering small satellites up to Earth orbit. For payloads up to fifty pounds or so, the supergun will cut launch costs by almost ninety percent. Anyway, Tom, what about the cannon?"

"Among the various propellants you looked at, wasn't there one you threw out because it was violently toxic?"

Mr. Swift nodded. "L-sixteen. It also made so much smoke, it blackened—" His eyes widened. "Tom, I think you're onto something!"

"A few grains of the stuff must have got into the regular waste that Sandra and I used."

"Hmm." Mr. Swift considered that for a moment. "You know, our Hazardous Materials division has a proud record. So when

I find the idiot who was stupid or careless enough—'' He said no more, but the angry glitter in his eyes implied that someone would soon be looking for another job.

"Well, all's well that ends well," Sandra declared.

"I'm not so sure it *has* ended," Tom told her. He went to the door and opened it. "All right, Rick, you can come in now."

Rick Cantwell went right to Sandra's bedside. "Are you okay?" he asked anxiously.

"Of course," Sandra replied. She asked innocently, "What makes you think I'm not?"

"Well, I—'' Rick was not sure how to answer that.

Mr. Swift chuckled and laid his hand on Rick's shoulder. "I think my daughter is just giving you a hard time. Isn't that right, Tom?"

"Sure." Tom flashed a quick grin, then became serious. "Rick, tell Dad and Sandra what you told me a little while ago."

"Oh, that." Rick looked embarrassed. "It's too weird. In fact, I'm beginning to wonder if I actually saw it or just imagined it."

"Saw what?" Sandra asked.

Rick sighed. "After I broke down the jet cycle, I went over to the Volatiles Test lab because I was curious to see what you and Tom were up to. Anyway, I had just left Administration when I saw Tom dash by carrying you . . ."

He hesitated.

"*All* of it," Tom insisted.

Rick took a deep breath and turned to Mr. Swift. "They were moving so fast, I barely got a glimpse. And I only saw Sandra, because Tom was blur."

Mr. Swift blinked. "I beg your pardon?"

Sandra turned to her brother. "What is he talking about?"

Rick tried to explain again. "It wasn't your speed that made you a blur. Although it was for only a brief moment, I did see Sandra quite clearly. It was you, Tom. You were . . ."

"A blur," Mr. Swift prompted gently.

"Yes."

"So you didn't actually see Tom?" Mr. Swift asked.

Rick shook his head. "No." A sudden grin. "Come to think of it, it could have been anybody—or anything."

"Hey, let's not get carried away," Tom said. He turned to his father. "There's more, you know."

"There is?"

"Dad, just think about it." Tom began

to tick off points on his fingers. "One—I was apparently almost invisible; a blur as Rick said. Two—although I was carrying Sandra, I was running faster than an Olympic athlete. Three—although I have a pretty good memory, there is no way I could have remembered those override codes—"

"But you did," Sandra protested.

"And four—why did I pass out at the nurse's station?"

Rick snorted. "Because you were exhausted! I would have been."

"You would have been dead," Tom said with a laugh. Then, serious once more, he turned to his father. "It all happened, Dad, exactly as you heard. Yet after a physical effort that would practically kill any normal human being, I'm still here. Why?"

"I guess, Tom, this is one paradox *you* had better start solving," Mr. Swift said. He checked his watch. "Right now, I'm late for a meeting. I have to go."

"Can I run a few more fire suit tests?" Sandra asked.

His eyes twinkling, her father shook a finger at her. "Only if Rob—and an army of rescuers—is on hand," he said with mock severity. Then he was gone.

* * *

After she was released from the infirmary, Sandra talked Tom into submitting to a series of mental and physical aptitude tests. The results came out completely normal— or as normal as could be expected from a physically healthy teenager with Tom's mental abilities.

Sandra was completely mystified. "Tom, during that emergency you were superhuman! You had superstrength, superintelligence, superspeed—"

"Fast enough to be a blur," he interrupted dryly. "Perhaps even fast enough to outrun my own jet cycle."

Sandra shrugged. "I know that people can do amazing things during life-and-death situations. A woman lifting a car after it rolls over her little boy, for instance."

"You mean that what we normally use is only a tiny fraction of what we have. So what happened to that woman with the car—and me—was hysterical strength triggered by increased adrenaline flow. Is that what you're trying to tell me?"

"Right!" Sandra clapped her hands. "Your dear sister was in trouble, so your adrenal glands did their stuff, and you saved me from a fiery demise!"

"I think I had an even more important reason than that," Tom said solemnly.

"Oh? What could possibly be more important than saving my life?"

"Saving mine," Tom said, and ducked as she threw a cushion at him.

The next day, Sandra and Rick Cantwell took the fire suit to Jefferson High, where Sandra had already entered it in the school's annual science fair. She couldn't demonstrate the suit's properties by using a real fire, so she and Rick simply inflated the suit and mounted it on a stand. Next to the gleaming, mirror-finish invention, a video monitor was set to run a continuous tape loop that showed a manikin wearing the suit being lowered into a white-hot furnace. According to temperature readouts down the edge of the screen, the manikin remained perfectly cool in the three-thousand-degree heat.

Several participants had left their own exhibits and were already gathered around when Rick started the tape. One wide-eyed girl watched the suit readouts rise slowly to eighty degrees and then stop. She turned and touched the material of the suit. "The stuff's all slithery, like—"

"Like it's covered with oil?" Sandra suggested. She was eager to explain her invention. "It's a characteristic of the buckycloth. Think of it as something made from billions of molecular ball bearings.''

"Oh, sure," the girl muttered as she wandered back toward her own model of a cold-fusion power generator.

The big doors at the end of the display hall opened. Helped by Mandy Coster, Tom entered with his jet cycle.

"Hey, it's Tom Swift!" someone yelled, and suddenly even Sandra's spectacular display was abandoned as everyone moved toward Tom and his latest creation. A platform was already set up for his display, and he and Mandy had plenty of help as they pushed the big machine across the floor and up the ramp to its assigned location.

Rick stopped what he was doing and admired the paint job on the jet cycle. "Looks good, doesn't it?" he commented proudly to Sandra.

Sandra balled her fist and thumped him on the arm. "Are you here to help me or admire the competition?"

He laughed. "Help you, of course! Anyway, what competition? Tom's not entering the fire bike. It's just a courtesy exhibit."

"Fire bike?"

"Well, it's—" Rick looked sheepish. "I coordinated the colors to make it look like a fire bike."

"Coordinated?" Sandra looked across the aisle at the garish jet cycle, then back at Rick and his purple jacket and brown pants. "Remind me to give you a few tips about color coordination."

Rick pretended his feelings were hurt as he and Sandra continued to swap friendly insults. Sandra's playful punch hadn't gone unnoticed by Tom and Mandy, who stopped polishing the jet cycle's turbofan housings and looked across.

"What's going on?" Mandy called.

Sandra pointed at the jet cycle. "The colors." She jerked her thumb at Rick. "He says they're coordinated!"

To Tom's annoyance, Mandy promptly responded with a mischievous "You're kidding!"

Tom glared across at Rick. "If I hadn't listened to you and your fancy ideas, my bike would have been a more reasonable color."

Mandy asked curiously, "What color, Tom?"

"Oh, I don't know. Black, I suppose."

Both girls laughed.

Tom and his friends continued to talk back and forth. As they did, Tom noticed another exhibit, across the aisle from his and a little farther down. The exhibit belonged to Leo Campbell, and Tom also noticed the frequent glances that Leo cast in the four friends' direction.

Tom had long suspected that Leo had a thing about Sandra. He'd caught him sneaking looks at his sister, then shifting his gaze if anyone caught him. Tom knew that skinny, shy Leo rarely got up the nerve to talk to Sandra. Although quite smart and a member of the Jefferson High basketball team, Leo lacked confidence. It didn't help that his classmates tended to address him as Beanpole. That made him even more shy and blundering around girls, and especially Sandra. Talking to her only made him stammer more. Now he was watching Sandra from the corner of his eye and looking thoroughly miserable as he continued to work on his computer display.

Earlier, Tom's curiosity had got the better of him. He had got permission to look at all of the science fair applications. Leo's had been very impressive.

The core of Leo's computer exhibit was a software program that he had designed to interface with 911 emergency calls. His system instantly identified the location of the caller on a monitor. It was a brilliant idea that had the potential to save lives and property. Nevertheless, Tom suspected that Leo underestimated just how good his project was.

A few of Leo's classmates didn't have a high opinion of him, either. Bart Heinster and Kevin Dekalle were two of them. Tom couldn't help overhearing them discuss a particularly nasty practical joke as they watched Leo from behind an adjacent exhibit.

"Isn't he a klutz?" Kevin sneered as Leo knocked a box on the floor, then dropped it again as he went to pick it up.

"He's a klutz, all right," Bart agreed nastily. "Got the disk?"

Kevin patted his pocket. "Got it."

Bart licked his lips like a jackal eyeing a piece of meat. "I tell you, Kevin, I am looking forward to this. Beanpole Campbell is about to provide all of us hardworking students with a comedy break." Robbie laughed in anticipation and gave Bart a loud high five.

Tom had never been fooled by Bart's phony friendliness and knew that he hated to play second fiddle to anyone—especially an apparent wimp like Leo Campbell. Despite Bart's best efforts, even when he cheated, which Tom suspected was often, Leo always seemed to edge Bart in grades as well as the things that mattered most to Bart—basketball and computers.

Leo had wandered off in the direction of the refreshment tables at the far end of the room. With a great show of casualness, Bart and Kevin walked along the aisle to Leo's display. Leo had left his system turned on. While Kevin stood in front of it and made sure no one came too close, Bart examined the setup.

"Gimme!" Bart whispered urgently. After accepting the disk from Kevin, he popped it into an appropriate slot, tapped some keys, and then waited for the virus to establish itself. After a few seconds, the machine beeped softly. Bart popped out the disk and touched Kevin on the shoulder. "Okay, let's get out of here."

When they were safely outside, Kevin asked, "Tell me again what that virus is going to do?"

Bart grinned with enormous satisfaction. "You'll just have to wait and see. I can tell you this much, though. Although Beanpole may think he's good with computers, he's not as good as the master." Bart tapped himself on the chest. "Tomorrow, right in front of everyone, Leo Campbell is going to get the surprise of his life!"

3

At TEN A.M. THE NEXT MORNING, TOM Swift, Sr., officially opened the science fair. As one of the fair's main sponsors, and as employer of some of the brightest people in the community, Mr. Swift had been asked to open the fair in previous years, and had always refused because of unavoidable commitments. This year Tom had asked his father to schedule just a half hour of his time for the fair, and Tom senior had not disappointed him.

Not given to long-winded speeches, and eager to see some of the work of the next generation of scientists before he departed to host a delegation of business people who were in town to view Swift Enterprises' latest line of industrial robots, Mr. Swift made a few appropriate remarks and then descended from the speaker's platform to begin a fast tour of the exhibits.

Hundreds of people were already crowding the aisles. In addition to the participants and their family members, other students, teachers, a lot of casual visitors, and several representatives of the media, including a TV crew, and radio and newspaper reporters, were there. Not unexpectedly, the aisles around Tom's jet cycle were jammed with people craning their necks to get a glimpse of it.

Like his father, Tom wanted to view the other exhibits. But he was so occupied with answering questions, he wasn't sure he would be able to get away. Mandy kept coming over, but this was one occasion when Tom would rather have had Rick around. Other than Tom himself, no one was more familiar with the bike's technical specifications. But Rick was helping Sandra. Across the aisle, the gleaming fire suit on its elevated pedestal was almost as eye-catching as the jet cycle and was attracting lots of visitors.

Rick knew that Sandra could handle her exhibit perfectly well without him, but the suit and its miraculous ability to keep out intense heat fascinated him. From time to time he glanced toward Tom's exhibit, wondering if he was really needed over there.

Meanwhile, Tom was being quizzed by a tall man in expensive-looking clothes. Although the man was polite enough, Tom was immediately suspicious.

"You can fly anywhere on that thing?" the man asked.

"Give me a couple feet of clearance all around," Tom declared proudly, "and I can take it down a well."

"What about noise? Those turbofans look pretty big to me."

"I know. But that's because they were designed to be quiet. The turbines are low-rev bypass type, sort of scaled-down versions of those used in the big jets like 747s. The thrusters and steering jets are low velocity, and there's lots of sound insulation. If I came down on top of you, you would feel the draft before you heard the bike."

"Is it hard to fly?"

"One half-hour lesson, and anyone should be able to operate it as well as I do." Tom pointed at the hand controls. "The left grip controls horizontal direction and speed, the right grip vertical direction and rate of rise or descent." Tom indicated a small box mounted between the grips. "The latest seven eighty-six microprocessor. While the most expensive personal computer you can buy today has a main chip with about a million and a half transistors, this baby has twenty million. It's what makes the bike do exactly what the rider wants. Without the microprocessor, the bike would be so unstable, even the hottest jet jockey could never fly it."

"Fly by wire," the man commented.

Tom frowned. The man's familiarity with the ability of a computer to accept human instructions and translate them into the thousands-per-second tiny adjustments that made the jet cycle flyable suggested he was from Swift Enterprises. Tom didn't recognize him, though. "Something like that," he replied cautiously.

The man nodded. "Very ingenious, Tom. Perhaps I can persuade you to give me a demonstration sometime."

"Perhaps," Tom said as he watched the man go.

Sandra came over. "Who was that?"

"I don't know. But he seemed to know his stuff."

"Maybe." She shivered. "He looked kind of creepy."

"He didn't leave his name," Tom said. "But he's got 'industrial spy' written all over him. That's sinking pretty low, when the competition comes to steal ideas from a high school fair."

Sandra nodded in agreement. "Stealing from amateurs is about as low as you can get. Of course," she added with a smile, "you're no amateur."

"And," Tom said, returning her smile, "I've already applied for patents on the key components and the new jet fuel formula. So he can look and admire all he wants. The jet cycle is mine, legally protected. No one can steal it from me now."

Meanwhile, many people walked by Leo's display. Some stopped and asked questions. Leo did his best to answer them, although he was convinced he sounded like a dull textbook. Most of the visitors may have thought so, too, because they rarely stayed long. There was one elderly man, however, who took the time to read one of Leo's photocopied leaflets.

"At the instant a 911 call is made, your equipment will identify the caller's phone number and street address?"

Leo nodded. "Yes, sir."

"You are obviously tapped into Emergency Services. Is that legal?"

"I have their permission." Which was true, although it was only for the day of the fair.

"Can you turn it on and show me?"

Leo shuffled his feet. "Well, actually, I'd rather wait until after the judging. But if you can come around as soon as that's over—"

The elderly man shrugged and slipped the leaflet into his inside pocket. "Unfortunately, I have to go. But perhaps, young man, you and I can talk about your project when you are less—ah—preoccupied."

I guess he wasn't really interested, Leo said to himself. Either that, or the old guy was put up to it. That's just the sort of thing Bart Heinster would pull on me.

Just then the PA clicked on. "Ladies and gentlemen, will all participants please return to their exhibits. The judges will commence their rounds in five minutes."

There was a minor flurry of activity as the refreshment tables were abandoned and anxious participants hurried back to their displays. Leo turned on his computer and monitor, then sat nervously and waited for the judges to arrive.

Leo looked toward the jet cycle. Tom Swift wasn't in sight, but Rick was there explaining something to a bystander. Then

Leo turned his attention back to Sandra's exhibit, but only Mandy was there.

Leo was instantly worried. If Sandra wasn't present when the judges arrived at her exhibit, she would be automatically disqualified. He stood on his toes and tried to see her among the crowds.

"Hi, Leo," Sandra said.

Startled, Leo swung around. She was just a couple of feet from him, looking curiously at his exhibit. "S-Sandra," he stammered. "Hi."

"What does it do?" she asked.

"It—er—" Instead of explaining, Leo thrust one of his leaflets into her hand.

Sandra seemed to only glance at the leaflet, but Leo knew she could speed read.

"This is great!" Sandra said. "Does it really work?"

Leo took a deep breath. "Of course."

"That's wonderful. Are you going to demonstrate it?"

He nodded vigorously. "Wh—when the judges come." Leo looked at her hopefully. "Will you be here when they do?"

She smiled, and Leo's heart leapt. "If I can."

He gestured. "You'd better get back. The judges will be here soon."

"Okay." Sandra turned to go, then stopped. "Leo, there are a couple of inseparables named Bart and Kevin. Do you know them?"

Leo nodded. "Sure. Bart Heinster and Kevin Dekalle. They're both on the basketball team, and Bart is pretty good with computers."

"Well, I saw them sneaking around your exhibit," Sandra continued. "Any idea why they would do that?"

"Just interested, I guess." Leo did his best to sound convincing.

"I hope you're right," Sandra said, but she looked doubtful.

As she hurried back to her own exhibit, Tom crossed the aisle to her. "What was that about?" he asked.

"What was what about?"

"You were talking to Leo Campbell. I'd be careful if I were you."

"Come on, he's just a pussycat. Since when did you get so interested?"

Tom took a deep breath. "I'm pretty sure Leo's got a crush on you."

To his surprise, Sandra merely smiled. "I know," she said.

Finally the three judges approached Leo's exhibit. They had just spent a long time at Sandra's display, but Leo didn't mind that. If Sandra won the grand prize, it would give him an excuse to congratulate her.

The first judge looked at the number above Leo's display, then consulted his list. "Leo Campbell?"

"Yes, sir."

"Please describe, in your own words, what you have here."

"It's a 911 interface, designed to instantly identify the source of any 911 call."

The judge looked impressed. "If your system works, it could save many lives. Can you give us a demonstration?"

"Glad to." Leo sat at the keyboard and tapped out the code that would connect his computer with Emergency Services.

A small, interested crowd had followed the judges. Among them was Sandra Swift. Even Tom and Rick Cantwell were there. At the back of the crowd, barely able to stifle their smirks, Bart and Kevin waited.

The monitor screen illuminated as Leo said, "This will display a street map with a flashing marker, indicating a 911 emergency caller's street address and phone number."

But instead of a grid of Central Hills's

streets appearing, a simple legend scrolled across the monitor:

"This call was placed from a phone booth located in North America on planet Earth. If you wish further information, please consult your local psychic."

4

AT FIRST THERE WAS A SHOCKED SILENCE.
Then the judges, the spectators, Tom and
Rick, and even Sandra, burst out laughing.
Only Leo didn't think the message was funny.

But Tom's mirth quickly evaporated
when he saw how upset Leo was. Tom
knew who was responsible. Turning, he
could see Bart and Kevin doubled over at
the back of the crowd. If anyone needed to
be squashed, it was those two. Leo Campbell had always been an ideal target for their
nasty tricks, and now they had outdone
themselves.

Tom looked for Leo and caught a brief
glimpse of him blundering away through the

36

crowd. Tom realized he must have felt so embarrassed that he wanted to get away from everyone.

"Tom, where did Sandra go?" It was Rick, looking about as ashamed as Tom felt.

"I don't know. Did she say anything?"

"Something about stopping a hurt. Was she talking about Leo?"

Tom sighed. "Yes, I suspect she was. Why don't we find Mandy and head back to my display."

"There she is," Rick said, waving.

The three of them made their way to the jet cycle exhibit and waited for Sandra.

When Sandra returned, she found them seated in a silent row on the edge of the display.

Tom looked hopefully up at his sister. "Did you find him?"

Sandra wearily flopped down next to her brother. "I think he's left the school."

"It was so cruel!" Mandy cried angrily. "Leo must have worked so hard, and then to be disqualified."

"Listen," Tom said. "Why don't we take another look around the big hall, just in case Leo is still here."

Privately, Tom agreed with Sandra that Leo had left the school, but he wanted to keep the two girls busy while he and Rick had it out with Bart Heinster. They split up to look for him.

Rick found Bart and Kevin at the refreshment tables. Rick immediately slapped Bart on the back, hard enough to cause him to choke. "What you did to that creep was great! Best laugh I've had in a long time!"

Bart smiled nervously. Rick was a big guy with muscles on top of muscles. "You liked it?"

It wasn't exactly an admission, so Rick tried again. "Was that what you call a virus?"

"Best thing he's ever done," Kevin declared, ignoring his friend's warning look. "Thought it up in no time at all. Didn't you, Bart?"

Rick lowered his head and whispered confidentially to Bart, "Tom Swift has been bugging me for a long time. Can we go somewhere quiet, so you can give me a few ideas on how to drop him a million feet? You know, with something along the lines of what you did to Beanpole?"

"Well . . ." Bart couldn't resist an opportunity to spike one of the most popular kids in the school. "I do have a few ideas," he admitted. "Trouble is, most of them are illegal."

"Illegal? Would that stop you?"

"It never stopped Bart before," Kevin put in. "He's into the school's computer, aren't you, Bart? Test results and everything."

"Shut up!" Bart snarled. "Your blabbing will wreck everything."

Rick lifted his hands. "Okay, okay. I won't talk if you don't." He pointed. "Let's go into that room and discuss it further. Okay?"

They went into the empty room, and Rick pulled the door closed behind them. Then, while Rick remained with his back to the door, Tom Swift rose from behind the desk where he had been hiding.

"Hello, Bart. Hi, Kevin."

Bart and Kevin looked nervously at the door. Rick smiled at them. "Gotcha," he said.

"So they took the bait, huh?" Tom asked.

Rick's smile grew broader. "Hook, line, and sinker. Bart would love to take you down a peg or two."

"Like he did to Leo Campbell?"

"Something like that." Rick held up his wrist and pointed to his large, thick-banded diver's watch. "I got it all on tape."

Bart barked a rude laugh. "I'm not falling

for that one. No one has a tape recorder that small."

Now it was Rick's turn to laugh. "I do—courtesy of my best friend, Tom Swift."

Bart and Kevin exchanged nervous glances as Rick pressed a knob on the side of the watch and their voices played back loud and clear.

Utterly defeated, Bart slumped back. "They'll kick me out of school." Then, horrified, he said, "My dad will make me go to work!"

Suddenly realizing what was going on, Kevin looked from his friend to his captors. "They won't kick *me* out of school, will they?" Pointing at Bart, he whined, "I mean, I'm not like him. I don't know anything about computers!"

"All right," Bart said. "What are you going to do?"

"Well, now . . ." Tom pretended to consider for a moment. Then, as if hit by a revelation, he snapped his fingers. "Tell you what, Bart. It's what *you* are going to do."

When the four came out of the room, Tom and Rick had broad smiles on their faces. Bart and Kevin looked extremely unhappy. Rick helped Tom escort their victims up the steps to the main platform, then returned to the floor while Tom turned on the mike and announced:

"Ladies, gentlemen, guests, and fellow students. Bart Heinster and Kevin Dekalle have something they want to say."

The crowd hushed. At one side of the room, Sandra and Mandy looked toward the platform with astonishment.

"What's Tom up to?" Mandy whispered.

Sandra shushed her. "We'll soon find out."

Bart slunk to the mike and said hoarsely, "I wish to humbly apologize to Leo Campbell. I installed the virus that wrecked his demonstration."

"It was a cruel and stupid trick," Tom whispered.

"It was a cruel and stupid trick," Bart repeated, almost gagging on the words.

Then it was Kevin's turn. "Sorry," he mumbled.

"You can go now," Tom said cheerfully, and watched as Bart and his accomplice shambled toward the door. From the hostile looks following them, Tom suspected those two would have a rough time at school for a while.

As Tom came down and joined Rick, the two girls ran up to them. "What was that about?" Sandra demanded.

"You heard," Rick said, trying to hold back a smile. "They apologized for what they did to Leo."

Sandra peered suspiciously at Rick. "How did you get them to do that?"

"It was easy," Tom replied, "once we got them to confess their sins into a tape recorder." He looked around. "No one's found Leo yet?"

Sandra shook her head. "He's long gone."

"Then perhaps we'd—"

Tom was interrupted as the principal of Jefferson High stepped up to the microphone. "Now for the awards, ladies and gentlemen. But first a few remarks from the mayor of Central Hills, the honorable Bart Heinster, Sr.!"

Fortunately, the mayor had long been aware that his only offspring was riding for a fall. If, at the cost of a little dignity, Bart junior had learned a valuable lesson, then Bart senior was content. Nevertheless, as he stared at Tom and Rick in the crowd, and wondered what they had on his son, the mayor decided to let those two know he did not approve of their methods—whatever they were.

"I hope that what I just witnessed does not mark the start of a trend. No matter what the justification, there are some forms of—ah"—he coughed—"persuasion that solve nothing."

After a moment, Tom whispered with a grin, "It's okay, Rick. I think you can un-cringe now."

Cautiously Rick uncoiled as the mayor launched into a speech about "the incredible promise of *you,* the next generation of scientists."

When he was finished, the principal rose to announce the twelve winners.

Amid the cheers and whistles of their friends and supporters, each in turn came up to receive a plaque and cash award from the mayor.

Finally the mayor himself announced the grand award. "For her exhibit, Fire Suit—"

The hall erupted with applause.

"Sandra Swift!"

Sandra accepted hugs and kisses from Rick, Mandy, and her brother, then made her way between yelling and screaming students to accept the award.

"Would you like to say something?" the mayor asked as he presented the award.

Sandra nodded and moved closer to the mike. Her eyes were moist. "There was a girl who was our schoolmate. Many of you knew her. Her name was Joy Marney, and she died in a fire. This"—Sandra held up the award—"is for her."

There was no applause, but the respectful silence was the best tribute Sandra could have imagined for her dead friend.

After a few moments, Sandra asked the mayor, "Can I say something else?"

"Of course," he replied.

Sandra went back to the microphone. "Leo Campbell, I hope you can hear me. I want to say how sorry I am for the terrible thing that was done to you. I also want to say—to everyone who is listening as well as to you, Leo—that if your equipment had been working as it should have when the judges came around, then it's possible that this honor would have been yours."

Leo did not hear Sandra because he was at home. He was living alone, as he did every spring when his mother spent a month with her sister in Montana.

Local newscasts announced the awards and even repeated Sandra's generous statement, but in Leo's house the radio was off. The phone repeatedly rang as the four friends took turns calling him, but Leo ignored it. Instead, he was forgetting his troubles amid the fantasy worlds of his enormous collection of comic books.

Leo had always equated Sandra with his favorite female heroine, Sky Sue. With her brilliant intellect and superfast aerospace flyer, *Sue's Bullet,* Sky Sue never had any problem doing all the things comic book heroines do best—protecting the innocent, helping the downtrodden, and always making sure the bad guys got what they deserved.

Sky Sue's faithful and competent assistant, Gavin Grange, was always at Sue's side when she needed him. As far as Leo was concerned, there wasn't much difference between Gavin and Tom Swift. Leo was convinced that Sandra was the real genius of the Swift family, not that publicity hound she had for a brother.

So what does a guy have to do to attract the attention of a popular girl like Sandra? Leo asked himself. Sky Sue, for instance, might pat the head of an oaf such as Leo "Beanpole" Campbell, but never *ever* would she go out with him. On the other hand, if a handsome hero like Major Stargo Hawk came along . . .

In that unlikely event, even Rick Cantwell would find himself out in the cold!

Leo's eyes glazed as he imagined himself as Stargo: discoverer of undersea civilizations, time traveler, and nemesis of count-less master criminals. Of course, as Sky Sue had her *Bullet,* Stargo Hawk had his Unitrans-grator. Even Tom Swift had a jet cycle—

Leo blinked and sat bolt upright in his chair. Unnoticed, his comics slid from his lap to the floor. Why is it that only fictional characters do wonderful things? he thought. Why not real people? Why not Leo Campbell?

Leo moved his standing lamp to the back of the room, opposite the big dresser mirror. Then he stood in front of the light so that if he squinted in just the right way, he could see only his outline framed by the light. Stargo Hawk had a secret identity—a be-spectacled major in charge of a military storage depot. So did Sky Sue, as legal sec-retary Sue Smith. So why not a hero who was also high school student Leo Campbell?

Leo pulled in his stomach and thrust back his shoulders. Now his silhouette did indeed look heroic, with his jutting jaw outlined by the light and the steely eyes of its owner con-cealed in the blackness. Add the superma-neuverability of the jet cycle, and he really *could* be a hero!

What do I have to lose? Leo thought. I've already been embarrassed in front of the whole school and in front of Sandra.

Leo picked up a comic from the floor. Major Stargo Hawk had just finished one of his adventures, and in the last panel on the front page, he was celebrating his triumph with a "Stargo Leap."

Leo's heart swelled as he looked at the airborne figure with arms outstretched, head back, and legs flexed for landing.

I will have a reason to leap like that, Leo vowed.

5

S ANDRA SWIFT COULDN'T SLEEP. AFTER A restless couple of hours, she put on her robe, padded to Tom's room, and knocked softly on the door.

Almost instantly the door opened. Tom was fully dressed in outdoor clothes.

"Tom, it's one A.M.! Where are you going?"

He grinned at her. "Why are you up and around at this unearthly hour?"

She gestured helplessly. "Couldn't sleep. Kept thinking of poor Leo."

"Yeah."

"You, too?"

He nodded. "He still won't answer the

phone, so I've decided to go over to his place. Want to come?"

She hesitated. "What do we do when we get there?"

"I don't know. But I'm sure I'll think of something—even if it's only to turn around and drive home again."

Sandra fondly patted his cheek. "Smart planning, brother dear. Sure, I'll come."

Meanwhile, Leo was scared. But he found that if he thought only of Sandra, he could conquer his fear.

After putting on dark clothing, Leo had driven his old pickup truck to the school. The night was blustery, with frequent sheets of driving rain, as he drove around the back of the school and parked behind the auditorium that housed the science displays. The security guard was huddled in a doorway, listening to a rock station on his pocket radio.

Like many of the students, Leo knew a few of the secret ways to get into the school. One was a manhole behind a screen of bushes next to the gymnasium. Leo ran from shadow to shadow until he dived behind the bushes. For a few moments he huddled close to the ground until he was sure the guard hadn't noticed him. Using a tire iron, he then pried back the manhole cover and dropped into a service tunnel below. After he replaced the cover, it was an easy run through the dimly lit tunnels and then into the school through a janitor's closet near the auditorium.

So far it had been astonishingly easy. Not quite as scared now as he had been when he started, Leo quietly entered the big, shadowed display area. Being careful not to disturb anything, Leo finally arrived at Tom Swift's display.

Even in the gloom, the flame-painted machine looked spectacular.

Despite the use of space-age materials that made the jet cycle much less heavy than it appeared, Leo needed all his strength to pull it off its stand and wheel it down the ramp to the floor. Then he pushed the big bike along the central aisle until he reached the double doors at the end of the auditorium that opened onto the street. He cautiously opened one of the doors and peered outside. It was raining again, and the streetlights reflected off glistening puddles of water. Leo's pickup was barely visible in the shadows a few feet away.

Leo ran to the pickup, lowered the tailgate, and carefully placed the heavy planks he had brought along to make a ramp. Then he went back to get the jet cycle.

Even with the pickup's manual winch, it took him several minutes to get the cycle loaded and secure beneath a tarpaulin.

Then Leo ran back to close the auditorium's doors, but just as he reached them, the almost full moon slid into a patch of clear sky between the rain clouds. A beam of pale radiance shone through the still open doors and illuminated a glittering shape that was almost ethereal among the other displays.

It was Sandra's fire suit.

It was awesome—and he knew he had to have it.

Leo's house, as Tom had expected, was in darkness when he and Sandra arrived.

"What now?" Sandra asked as they stood on the porch. They had knocked and rung the doorbell, without result.

Tom shrugged. "He's either in a deep sleep or ignoring us, or he's not home."

"Now, that is a smart bit of deduction," his sister said.

"Actually, I think it's more likely that Leo has gone somewhere." Tom pointed at wet tire ruts in the driveway. "I suspect that's where he normally parks his pickup."

"Which means he could be anyplace between here and China. So let's go home and get some sleep.''

"No.''

"No?''

Tom produced a key from his pocket. "A few months ago, Leo talked me into coming over and helping him set up a new computer system. It wasn't much of a job, but he was so grateful, he insisted I take this key in case I wanted to use his system for one of my projects. I didn't have the heart to tell him I have access to one of the best mainframes in the country, so I took the key.''

Tom opened the door. "Go home if you want, but one way or another, I intend to find out what's going on with Leo.''

Despite the key, Sandra still felt like a trespasser as she followed Tom into the dark house. Then she took a deep breath and squared her shoulders. "Okay, Tom, let's find out what happened to Leo.''

Almost as if he were in a dream, Leo reentered the auditorium and went to the suit. He lifted it off its stand, deflated it, folded it, and then carefully carried it out of the building as though it were something sacred. Not until he was back in his pickup and turning into the street outside the school did Leo realize the awful thing he had just done.

He had stolen from Sandra!

He had also stolen from Tom Swift, but somehow that didn't seem as important. Leo almost turned the pickup around so he could return the glistening suit, which he had placed on the seat next to him. Instead, he continued driving out of town and up into the hills.

The miles rolled by until the pickup emerged from beneath the rain clouds into a cool desert night. Finally Leo pulled off the graveled road and parked next to a dried-up streambed.

Did he want to try the bike?

Yes, of course he did. But first the suit!

Leo didn't know that Tom Swift had already fire-tested the suit. Instead, he persuaded himself that he would be performing a great service for Sandra. After all, he did have a video camera in the pickup. With the kind of visual record he was about to produce, he would return the suit and be a hero at the same time!

Leo mounted the camera on the lowered side window of the pickup. Then he scrambled down into the arroyo and gathered armfuls of brush and wood, which he dumped in a pile about a hundred feet from the pickup. Next he put on the fire suit. Flexible and stretchable, it slid easily over his skinny limbs and body like a second skin. He pulled the hood over his head, and after a few seconds of fumbling, figured out how it snapped into position on the neck ring.

Finally, after he started the camera, Leo lit the fire. The wood was bone-dry and quickly flared up.

Gingerly at first, then with growing confidence, Leo approached the flames and finally stepped completely into the fire. Although the fire wasn't very large, Leo was sure it was hot enough to fry an unprotected human being. Surrounded by the flames, he crouched down and remained in a squatting position for nearly ten minutes, until the fire consumed itself. To Leo's amazement, the suit kept him cool and unharmed.

What would Stargo Hawk do now?

With a whoop, Leo leapt up in triumph from the remains of the fire—and to his astonishment soared nine feet into the air. As he landed, he flexed his knees and leapt again, this time to at least twice his own height before he alighted next to the pickup. Exhilarated, Leo began to run—and found himself circling the pickup like a human whirlwind.

"Is this place the same as when you were here before?" Sandra whispered. She made a face at the sink full of unwashed dishes in the kitchen.

"I hope so," Tom replied as he led the way up the stairs to Leo's room. The computer and its peripherals were on a table across from the unmade bed. In one corner was a big chair with an untidy pile of comics strewn on the floor next to it. While Sandra went over and checked the comics, Tom turned on the computer and sat down at the keyboard.

He quickly accessed a directory of files. There was a clutter of items on the hard disk: games, a word-processing program, spread sheets, and a large subdirectory labeled 911. When Tom tried to get into that directory, the computer promptly asked for a password.

Tom grunted disgustedly and turned off the machine. "If I had the time, I could probably crack this thing."

Sandra turned from her inspection of the comics. "Would it do any good?"

"I doubt it." Tom joined her. "What have you found?"

"The Adventures of Sky Sue," Sandra read aloud from the cover of one comic.

Tom picked up another comic. *"Stargo Hawk and His Unitransgrator."* As he tossed the comic aside, his eye was caught by a wall of shelves completely stacked with comics. "I had forgotten. Leo must have the biggest collection in town."

"I'd rather collect bottle tops," Sandra said.

"Don't knock it. Some collectors would pay a fortune for this lot."

Sandra shrugged. "Let's go home, okay? Before someone notices we're here and dials"—she shuddered—"nine-one-one."

Leo leaned against the side of the pickup. He felt like a spring that was only partly unwound, as if he could still run like the wind and leap like a deer.

He looked down at himself, and at the fire suit that covered him. The stars were bright, yet Leo was sure the sparkles in the material were more than just reflections. It was as if the suit had a life of its own, separate from the person within it.

It *must* have been the suit. Without it, he had been Leo "Beanpole" Campbell, the laughing stock of Jefferson High. With it, he was superhuman!

Carefully Leo began to remove the suit. He removed the hood, then slid down the fastening that opened the front of the mirac e garment. He felt strangely giddy, and his .eart was thumping like crazy. He found himself taking enormous breaths, as if he could not get enough air. He tried to concentrate on what he was doing, but his fingers were like thick stumps, and his vision rippled as if he were looking through layers of turbulent water.

"Overdid it," he muttered. "Must have over—"

His eyes wide and sightless, Leo slowly toppled to the ground.

6

Leo struggled to his feet and clung groggily to the side of the pickup. Although his heart wasn't thumping hard anymore, and his head was clearing, he still felt as if he were recovering from a bad case of the flu.

He was also very hungry.

After munching on a stale chocolate bar that he found in the glove compartment, Leo pulled one arm out of the suit and checked his watch. As near as he could tell, he had been unconscious for almost an hour, but as he took deep breaths, he began to feel much better.

It must have been nervous tension, he decided. Anyone would flake out after what he'd been through in one day.

Leo finished removing the suit, carefully refolded it, and placed it on the seat in the pickup. Then, after he unbracketed and stowed the video camera, he went around to the back of the pickup and climbed aboard. He pulled back the tarpaulin and stared at the gleaming jet cycle.

Did he dare to try it?

Leo still didn't feel one hundred percent, but he figured he could sit on the bike and start it up.

He had heard Tom Swift brag about the simplicity of the controls and had been there when Tom pointed out the various operating features of the hand grips. Starting the bike *was* easy—a simple switch was mounted on the top of the box between the grips.

Again Leo checked his watch. It was just after three A.M. He told himself, A few minutes. That's all I need.

He swung his long legs over the central frame and lowered himself onto the seat.

He touched the switch.

A thin whine slowly rose in intensity as the turbines ran up to speed, then came a gentle *whump* as the fuel ignited and dust swirled up from the bed of the pickup.

Leo muttered, "Left, horizontal. Right, vertical."

He cautiously twisted the right grip forward. The whine rose to a faint shriek, and the bike trembled. He twisted a little more. Slowly the jet cycle lifted. He twisted back, and the jet cycle hovered a few feet above the pickup. It began to drift sideways, so Leo adjusted the left grip to produce a compensating lateral thrust.

Leo found himself grinning like a fool. A child could fly this thing, he thought.

He began to circle and gain altitude. The pickup dropped below him until it was just a small, blocky shadow on the moonlit landscape.

Leo experimented. Up, down, forward, back, and sideways. As he gained confidence, he began to glide through the air with ease. He tried a speed run, then hurriedly throttled back when he realized he needed goggles. He played in the air like a young bird just discovering its wings, and with as much fun. For a few glorious minutes, Leo even forgot Sandra.

Finally he lowered the jet cycle back down onto the bed of the pickup. Although the truck bed was a small target, he found the operation ridiculously easy and barely felt the contact between the wheels and the truck bed. He touched the switch, and the turbines slowly whined into silence.

After he concealed the bike under the tarpaulin, Leo headed for home. He had driven farther into the desert than he'd thought, and as he finally descended into the outskirts of Central Hills, the eastern sky was already rimmed with crimson. So when Leo finally arrived home and stumbled indoors, all he wanted to do was sleep.

But first he decided to look at the videotape.

Tom shook his father awake. Bleary-eyed, Mr. Swift stared at his son. "Wh . . . what time is it?"

Tom glanced at his watch. "Nearly three."

"In the morning?"

Sandra nodded. "Sorry, Dad, but we need to talk to you."

Mr. Swift gingerly got out of bed in order not to wake his wife, motioning for Tom and Sandra to follow him out of the room. "This had better be good."

"We're worried about Leo Campbell," Tom told him.

"Campbell?" Mr. Swift sleepily searched his memory. "The boy whose exhibit was sabotaged?"

"Right," Tom said. "We were just over at his place."

"At this time of night? I bet he was happy to see you."

"He wasn't there."

"So we used a key and went in," Sandra said.

Mr. Swift's eyebrows rose. "A key? What kind of key?"

After Tom explained, his father said, "Somehow I don't think your entering his house in the middle of the night is what Leo had in mind when he gave you that key."

"Look, Dad," Sandra said. "We had a good reason. You didn't see Leo's face after that trick was played on him."

"So you entered his house in the middle of the night, just because of his"—Mr. Swift took a deep breath—"facial expression?"

"You still don't understand. I laughed when Leo's monitor came up with that silly message. So I feel sort of responsible for whatever might have happened to him."

"You're right, I don't understand. From what you told me about that incident, a lot of people laughed."

"I know they did. But . . ." Sandra bit her lip and looked embarrassed. "You see, Tom and I are pretty sure that Leo has a crush on me."

Thomas Swift, Sr., put one hand on his daughter's shoulder. "Look, I'm glad that you don't want to hurt his feelings, but you have to let Leo work this out for himself. For all you know, he's spending the night at a friend's. Still, why don't you tell me what you found at his home. Maybe we can make some sense out of it."

Leo ran the tape.

He watched himself walk into the fire and stay there, unharmed.

He watched himself take two enormous leaps. Leo figured the leaps would have astonished even Stargo Hawk.

Finally Leo's eyes widened with disbelief as he watched himself accelerate into a blur—and vanish.

He rewound the tape and viewed it again, this time in slow motion. As it ran, his bright, glittering figure became a confusing mixture of reflected motion. It was as if the suit were a collection of tiny mirrors that reflected the stars so that they resembled a tight, whirling cloud of fireflies. As he moved faster, the tiny points of light blended together. Finally, as the figure on the screen slowed, the points of light returned, and then, quite suddenly, the glittering familiarity of Sandra's fire suit.

Leo wanted to shout to the world, but by now fatigue had overwhelmed him. He closed his eyes and fell asleep, visions of superpowered heroes leaping in his head. In his sleep, Leo smiled.

"So what did you find in Leo's house?" Mr. Swift asked.

Tom shuffled his feet. "Not much, really. At least we didn't disturb anything."

"The place was a mess," Sandra declared.

Despite himself, Mr. Swift laughed. "All right, so it was a mess and you left it that way. "What else can you tell me?"

Tom shrugged. "His new computer is at the school, so the equipment in the house is pretty archaic. I turned it on, but the interesting stuff was protected with a password. Leo also has an enormous collection of comic books, and some of them were on the floor by his chair."

"Any comic books in particular?" Mr. Swift asked.

"*The Adventures of Sky Sue,* plus *The Further Adventures of Stargo Hawk and His Unitransgrator.*"

"What in heaven's name is a unitrans—?"

"Unitransgrator. It's sort of a cross between a jeep and a time machine."

"Sorry I asked," Mr. Swift grumbled. "Does any of this mean anything?"

Again Tom shrugged. "Hard to say." He began ticking off points. "First, Leo's science project gets sabotaged by a couple of low-life geeks. Second, we find Leo missing. Third, we find an impressive comics collection, with an emphasis on superheroes." Tom paused. "It could all add up to nothing," he continued. "But for some reason, warning bells are going off in my head."

Mr. Swift frowned. "Over the years I've learned to trust your intuition, Tom. But all that's really happened so far is that Leo spent a night away from home. Still, keep me posted on any further developments."

"Thanks, Dad," said Tom. He and Sandra quietly returned to their own bedrooms. Tom wasn't sure why, but he felt trouble brewing.

It was nearly noon when Leo finally stumbled out of bed.

He never slept late, not even on Sundays and not even when he had stayed up most of the night working on his 911 interface.

Leo was more than tired. He felt as if he hadn't slept for a month. Running on automatic, Leo staggered into the shower. From the shower he went to the breakfast table, where he stuffed himself with huge portions of juice, cereal, eggs and bacon, toast, and whatever else he could find to feed his insatiable appetite.

At least he wasn't hungry anymore, although he was still tired. He hit the sack for another couple of hours, and when he woke up again, he felt almost normal.

But he still didn't feel good enough to do dishes or clean house or even call a friend— if he had any. After all, it was only the day before that he had run away from the science fair like a scared rabbit. Who would want to talk to him?

If I could just get Bart and Kevin alone for a few minutes . . .

Leo knew he was fooling himself. There was no way he could wipe the floor with those two. Not unless he somehow acquired superhuman powers.

He went to the window and looked out at his pickup parked in the driveway. Tom Swift's jet cycle still rested beneath the concealing tarpaulin like an ungainly piece of furniture.

Leo thought about Stargo Hawk and then about Sky Sue.

There was no doubt that either of those two would be off and running if they had what Leo had. In fact, Leo couldn't think of any hero who had the dual advantage of incredible mobility *and* the ability to be invisible.

Leo turned from the window and wandered to his computer. He sat down, turned it on, and for a few moments stared bemused at the blank screen.

Come on, Campbell. It's time to put your money where your mouth is!

7

AFTER HOOKING UP THE BREADBOARD AR-rangement that was his prototype scanner, Leo entered the code that started his old computer scanning for 911 emergency calls. When a call was detected, he hoped it would be something more dramatic than a report that some kid's pet cat was stuck in a tree.

For several minutes the monitor displayed the simple legend *Searching*.

Suddenly there was a sound of a phone ringing. A map reappeared on the screen, along with a flashing marker and a full address and phone number.

"Emergency operator," said a crisp voice.

An elderly female voice said, "There's a burglar in the house!"

"What is your address, ma'am?"

"He told me he was the telephone repairman. Then he made me show him where I keep my nice things. Now I'm locked in the bedroom!"

"Ma'am, I need your address."

"My husband isn't at home. Please tell my husband to come home just as quickly as he can."

"Lady. Please. What is your address?"

Leo already had that information flashing crisp and clear on his monitor. He read the address: 2091 Sycamore.

He knew it well. When Leo was younger, he'd had a paper route along Sycamore. It was a street of large, expensive houses no more than a couple of miles to the north.

He even remembered number 2091. It had belonged to a nice elderly couple, Mr. and Mrs. Devinski. Leo especially remembered the Devinskis' friendly little dog, which had taken a liking to him and always wanted to play.

Leo started to reach for the phone, then hesitated. By the time the police got the message and were able to respond, the thief would be long gone with his loot. Poor Mrs. Devinski would have nothing to show for it except missing valuables and the memory of a terrible experience.

On the other hand . . .

Leo did not waste further time thinking about what, in the back of his mind, he had been daring himself to do, anyway. Instead, he ran out of the house to his pickup and whipped off the tarpaulin. It took only a minute to clamber into the fire suit and then start up the bike. As the turbines whined up to speed, Leo mentally checked the route he would follow. Fortunately, both his house and 2091 Sycamore were near the forested river valley, so he wouldn't have to fly over heavily populated areas.

Leo touched the throttle, and like an elevator, the jet cycle lifted into the sky.

Captain Invisible was on his way!

Leo steered the bike just above the river's surface, close to the left bank so that he remained in the tree shadows. To his right, on the other side of the river, the colors of spring were spectacular under the slanting rays of the evening sun. Soon he saw the marker he was looking for: a TV tower that he knew was across the river from Sycamore.

Leo touched the controls, and the bike ascended and banked left. He didn't climb completely over the trees, but flew just below the treetops, weaving his way like a great owl hunting its prey. Only a startled small boy saw the monster whir overhead.

Leo landed in a wooded area between the river and the property of 2091 Sycamore. As he touched down, he could see the house through the trees. It seemed quiet.

Leo stooped low and ran closer.

Suddenly he saw a faint flicker of something metallic and then a moving shadow.

Leo sealed the hood of the suit, took a deep breath, and then ran as fast as he could toward the house. To his disappointment, he did not move like greased lightning as he had in the desert. But as he weaved back and forth between the bushes and trees of the enormous garden, the suit's peculiar optical properties broke up Leo's running image so that he became just a vague hint of movement, inseparable from the gentle movement of vegetation rustling in the wind. Finally Leo dropped prone behind an ornamental trellis and waited.

Meanwhile, the thief was crouched low against the wall of the house. The job had taken longer than he anticipated, and he wanted to make sure there was no cop or eager-beaver neighbor waiting in ambush. More worrying was the dog bowl and empty leash hook labeled Wolf that he had seen in the kitchen on his way out.

Only big dogs were called Wolf, and the thief hated dogs of any size. Cautiously, gun in hand, he rose to his feet and prepared to run.

Suddenly a car door slammed. Then a shout: "Wolf! Come back here!"

The thief lifted his gun just as he heard the sound of skittering feet and then a dog's low growl. Suddenly an enormous hound skidded around the corner of the house.

The thief pulled the trigger—

Just as a frightening apparition appeared out of nowhere and knocked the gun upward as it fired.

Even the dog was scared. With a whimper, the big Irish wolfhound backed away as the glittering, goggle-eyed humanoid extracted the gun from the thief's trembling hand and tossed it aside. The thief just stood petrified as his terrible assailant took the bag of loot and carefully placed it on the ground.

"W-what are you?" the thief gasped.

"I am . . ." The muffled voice hesitated, then added with sinister emphasis, "he who brings vengeance!"

"Noo—" The thief's eyes rolled back

until only the whites showed. Then he collapsed.

At first, Mr. and Mrs. Devinski were also terrified when they saw what stood over the crumpled robber. Mr. Devinski, who had just brought Wolf home from the vet, was the first to realize that perhaps the bright-suited stranger intended no harm. He patted his wife's shoulder and said ressuringly, "I think it's all right, dear. Look at Wolf. He's not frightened."

Indeed, the dog had overcome his fear and was panting happily as he looked up at their savior with almost an adoring look in his big brown eyes.

Mrs. Devinski, in the same quavering voice Leo had heard when he intercepted the emergency call, ordered the big dog to her. "Come here, Wolf. Bring the bag."

The wolfhound lowered his shaggy head and sniffed the unconscious thief. Then he picked up the bag of loot in his jaws and carried it to his mistress. She knelt stiffly and looked inside the bag. It was all there: the silverware that had been given as a wedding present, an opal ring that had once belonged to her mother, a tiny ornate mirror that had been in her family for generations. When Mrs. Devinski looked up, her old eyes were filled with tears of gratitude.

"Thank you," she said.

The stranger said nothing.

Mr. Devinski asked daringly, "Perhaps you are a visitor from another world?"

Leo, who now knew that these were the nice people of his paper-route days, and that the great hound was the puppy who had always greeted him with a ball that he wanted Leo to throw, wished he could pull off the hood and make friends with them again. Instead, he remained silent.

"Wolf doesn't take easily to strangers. And you may not even be hu—" Mr. Devinski bit his lip.

There was the sound of a police siren. Leo turned to go.

"Please stay," Mrs. Devinski pleaded.

Mr. Devinski shook his head. "No, he has to go. The police won't understand."

They watched with their dog as the stranger faded away into the trees. Finally, when they could not see him anymore, a voice called, "Tell them Captain Invisible was here!"

On Monday morning Tom answered the phone. It was Mr. Dejonge, the science teacher who was the coordinator of the science fair.

"Tom, I know the fair was officially over

when it closed on Saturday evening, but why did you and Sandra have to be in such a hurry? I was hoping to give a few of my students a private viewing before the exhibits are removed."

"I'm, sorry, Mr. Dejonge, but I don't know what you're talking about. What exhibits?"

"Yours and Sandra's, of course. They're gone. I presume you took them yesterday—didn't you?"

"No, we didn't."

Upset, angry, and thoroughly bewildered, Tom finally got off the phone just as Rick arrived to drive him and Sandra to school. Still shrugging into his jacket, Tom climbed into the backseat behind Sandra and said breathlessly, "Sorry to tell you this, Sis, but your fire suit and my jet cycle have been stolen from the fair."

Sandra gasped. "No!"

Astonished, Rick looked back at his best friend. "Are you sure?"

"Mr. Dejonge just called and told me." Tom waved his hand forward. "Come on, Rick, let's get going!"

Rick's old Jaguar roared out of the driveway and turned toward town. "Anything else taken?" Rick asked.

"If it was, Mr. Dejonge didn't mention it."

Sandra turned on the car radio. "Perhaps there's something on the news."

She immediately picked up a local radio announcer who was breathlessly describing the mysterious doings on Sycamore.

". . . All we know so far is that a robbery at the Devinski residence at 2091 Sycamore was foiled by what Mr. Devinski described as a spaceman who appeared as if by magic out of thin air. The robber, who was taken to the Central Hills Hospital after apparently suffering a severe shock, is still not in any condition to make a statement. Seven-year-old Jimmy Covitt, who was playing nearby at the time, told our reporter he saw a 'dragon thing' fly through the trees at about the time the robbery was probably still in progress. The police remain close-mouthed about the whole affair, although Chief of Police Robin Montague did comment that she attaches little credence to Mrs. Devinski's insistence that after the spaceman disappeared, someone shouted, 'Tell them Captain Invisible was here.'

"So what does it mean, folks? Did it really happen, or does this mark the beginning of a new silly season? Is there such a person as Captain Invisible, and if so, is he our first extraterrestrial visitor? Stay tuned!"

As Sandra turned off the radio, she said sarcastically, "Compared to that inspired bit of reporting, a theft from a local school science fair does seem sort of uninteresting, doesn't it?"

Tom said, "Rick, stop the car."

"Sure." After they rolled to a stop, Rick leaned on the wheel and looked curiously at his friend. "I know you, Tom. What's on your mind?"

Tom gestured at the radio. "That broadcast. I think it's connected."

That startled Sandra. "No way!"

"I mean it. For instance, 'spaceman' could mean 'space-suited man.' Right?"

"So?"

"So what about the 'dragon thing'? Couldn't it be my jet cycle?"

Rick's eyes widened. "Wow. Which means the space suit is—"

"Sandra's fire suit."

Sandra bit her lip thoughtfully. "Tom, you could be right. But there is a catch, isn't there?"

"Such as?"

"The invisibility factor. How do you explain it?"

"Sandra, have you forgotten what Rick

told us at the infirmary—after that almost fatal experiment of ours?''

Rick's eyes widened with sudden recollection. ''That's right!''

Sandra whispered. ''It was when you ran with me to the infirmary. Rick said he didn't see you. Only me and a—''

'' 'Blur' was the word he used. Right, Rick?''

''Right,'' Rick echoed.

''Oh, Tom, this is ridiculous.''

Rick sighed exasperatedly. ''Look, will someone please tell me what this is leading up to?''

''I'll do better than that,'' Sandra said as she opened the glove compartment and began rummaging through a collection of old spark plugs, frayed wire, and other gadgets of a mysterious but used nature. ''Rick, have you got any string?''

''In my pocket,'' he replied.

''Now he tells me,'' Sandra said as she withdrew a dirty hand. She abruptly jabbed an elbow sideways, causing Rick to go *''whoof!''* ''Out of the car. Both of you!''

8

THEY WERE IN A RELATIVELY QUIET AREA just outside the town. Sandra led the way up a grassy bank, through a gate, and into an empty field. She found a smooth stone a couple of inches across, then produced a square of bright material that she wrapped around the stone.

"Buckycloth," she said. "I have a piece with me."

She took a length of string from Rick and firmly tied the end around the buckycloth-wrapped stone. Then she gave the string back to Rick.

"Swing it around your head," she ordered.

"Huh?"

Tom laughed aloud. "You're a genius! Rick, do as she says. I think you're about to get the surprise of your life."

"You're both mad," Rick muttered as he began to whirl the stone in a glittering arc.

For the first few swings, all they saw was a brightly wrapped stone. But as Rick got into a rhythm and the circles became faster, the wrapped stone began to flicker like an intermittent silver flame. Then, suddenly, it was simply not there—just a whirring vagueness barely visible at the end of the string. By this time, Rick's arm was getting tired and he began to slow down.

The vagueness became a circle of flickering silver . . . then a brightly wrapped stone.

Finally Rick held the string before him, the stone hanging innocently like a stilled pendulum.

Tom smiled and said, "If I hadn't seen it for myself, I wouldn't believe it. Rick, would you mind doing that again?"

Rick gave him the string. "No, Tom. You do it."

Rick watched with Sandra as Tom repeated the experiment, with the same unsettling result. When it was over, the three of them walked back to the car.

"That's incredible," Rick said as he

leaned on the steering wheel and stared at the empty road.

Tom nodded. "I know."

Sandra spread the piece of buckycloth on her knees. She realized now that in her haste to help provide a way to rescue people trapped in fires, she may have moved too quickly.

"Tom," she said, "my invention seems to have hidden properties."

Tom smiled at her. "Yes. It sure looks like you've got a tiger by the tail. Think of the possibilities. . . ."

He paused for a moment, then became deadly serious. "You know," he said, "I have a bad feeling about this."

"Why?" said Rick. "Afraid Sandra will win a Nobel Prize before you do?" he asked with a chuckle.

Sandra turned to him. "Please, Rick, this is no laughing matter. Tom, what's on your mind?"

Tom frowned. "I'm not sure, but let's consider recent developments. Leo disappears. Your fire suit and my jet cycle are stolen. A fantastic character appears from nowhere, acting like a superhero." He turned to Sandra. "Whether we like it or not, everything adds up."

Sandra nodded.

"You mean," said Rick, "that Leo stole your inventions and became a real-life comic book superhero?"

"Yes," said Sandra, "and that isn't the worst of it. We don't know how or why the buckycloth becomes invisible or what other hidden properties it may have. Or even how it affects the person wearing it. I should have tested it further. Tom, Rick—I think Leo's in big trouble."

They arrived at school in time to be summoned to the auditorium by a stout, red-faced detective. The detective, who was a recent transfer from a tough city precinct in which most of the kids he dealt with carried guns, chains, and knives, asked bluntly, "I'm Detective Karvetti. Are you Swift?"

"Yes," said Tom and Sandra simultaneously.

The detective glared at Sandra. "I'll get to you later, young lady."

Then, to Tom, "Do you know about the Captain Invisible robbery?"

"I know about the robbery that some character in a space suit *prevented,*" Tom said with a grin. "We heard it on the car radio as we came to school."

"Do you know what I think?"

Tom exchanged quick glances with Rick

and his sister. This guy was not exactly Mr. Geniality. "I think you're just about to tell us what you think."

The detective's face became even redder. "I think you're a spoiled rich kid who likes to get a rise out of hardworking law officers like me. Frankly, I wouldn't be surprised if it turns out that you stole your own flying gadget, dressed up in that silly fire suit gimmick, and then scared a couple of nice old people just so you could get a few kicks. Now, what do you think of that?"

Tom knew the detective was serious, and that it would be a mistake to laugh.

"Is that all?" he asked mildly.

"Not entirely. Calling yourself Captain Invisible suggests to me you're one of those bums who sits around and reads comic books all day. Do you read comic books, Mr. Swift?"

Comic books. That was an angle Tom hadn't thought of. "I've read a few," he admitted.

"Exactly what I thought." The detective rammed a stubby finger against Tom's chest. "I can't prove anything yet, but I will. Meanwhile, I'm going to see your father and suggest to him that he put you on ice until this case is resolved. I don't want you or any of your friends cluttering up this investigation with irresponsible antics."

"What irresponsible antics?" Mr. Swift asked as he hurried over, accompanied by the harried figure of the principal of Jefferson High. "I just heard about the robbery. Tom, Sandra, I'm so sorry. Who would do such a thing?"

"It wasn't me, Dad," Tom said.

"Of course not! Who would suggest—?"

Rick jerked his thumb at the detective. "Meet Detective Karvetti, Mr. Swift. He thinks that Tom took the bike and the fire suit so he could use them to terrorize some old people over on Sycamore."

"Well, Detective Karvetti, I could, of course, exercise my rights as a citizen and complain to Police Chief Montague about your rash accusations. On the other hand, it seems to me you would better serve your noble profession if you spent more of your time doing what your local colleagues already do so well, which is cooperating with citizens instead of antagonizing them."

After the now-subdued detective departed, a mob of reporters burst into the auditorium and quickly surrounded the little group.

"Mr. Swift, is it true that a foreign power

would like to get its hands on your son's jet cycle, and that its agents have recently been spotted in Central Hills?''

"No, it is not true.''

"What about the criminal element? Wouldn't the jet cycle be worth a lot of money to a lot of people?''

"Yes.''

"Sandra, what possible military uses do you see for the fire suit?''

"No comment,'' Sandra replied.

"Tom, is it true that you got the Captain Invisible idea out of a comic book?''

Tom just laughed and shook his head.

"Would it be possible to arrange a group photograph with the Swift and Devinski families together?''

"No!'' chorused the Swift family.

"Have you yet spoken to either of the Devinskis, Mr. Swift? And if so, what did they tell you about your son's involvement?''

"No. And Tom was *not* involved.''

Finally a few members of the school security team hustled the reporters out of the auditorium and off school grounds.

Meanwhile, Leo had gotten over the thrill of being Captain Invisible and began to face the facts. He had been disgraced in school, in front of all his classmates. He had broken into the school. He had stolen Tom's and Sandra's inventions. He had frightened a thief half to death.

It was too much. Events had gotten out of hand so quickly that Leo hadn't even had the time to stop and think things through. Now that he had, he was scared. But he knew what he had to do.

"Got to take the stuff back," he said aloud. "It's the only way out of this mess."

A little after two A.M. Tuesday morning, a glittering figure on a strange machine descended out of a dark, cloudy sky. It was quiet as Leo pushed the bike behind a screen of bushes at Jefferson High, and then ran to the manhole leading to the service tunnel.

As he had before, Leo padded through the service tunnel and then entered the school through the janitor's closet.

Leo entered the auditorium and walked over to his own display. He stopped and toyed with it for a few moments. His life would have been very different if those two clowns had not made him the buffoon of the school. He might even have won an award. Even Sandra . . .

Shaking his head and forgetting he had

just turned on his computer, Leo continued
to the loading doors.

He opened them carefully and looked out.
Still quiet. Still very dark.

Leo ran back to the bike and began to
push it toward the doors. Suddenly he was
illuminated in a bright beam of light. An amplified voice boomed from the blackness behind the beam:

"Stay where you are. You're under
arrest!"

The police!

Leo panicked. Without thought and with
only a desperate desire to escape, he
jumped onto the seat of the jet cycle and hit
the start switch. Within seconds the turbos
whined up to speed.

"Stop, or we'll shoot!"

Leo couldn't see anyone, only that glare
of light. He heard a *whump* as the fuel ignited. He twisted the right grip as far as it
would go. The bike shuddered and lurched
into the air.

Lift. Lift! *Lift!*

As the turbines built up thrust, the bike
began to move—forward at first, struggling
for height. But the bike was picking up
speed without gaining much altitude, and
Leo was blinded by the light.

Suddenly there was a surge of acceleration, a thump, and the jet cycle jerked. As he regained control, Leo looked below him. What he saw, illuminated in stark relief by the searchlight, he knew he wouldn't forget for the rest of his life.

A motorcycle, wheels still spinning, lying atop the sprawled body of a uniformed policeman.

Leo screamed into the night. "Sorry! I d-didn't mean it! Didn't m-mean it!"

9

WAKE UP! COME ON, SANDRA, WAKE UP!"

Tom, fully dressed, was at his sister's bedside. The clock indicated 2:55 A.M. Sandra sat up. "What happened?"

"I just got a call from Chief Montague. She's at the school. It seems Captain Invisible tried to raid the place."

Sandra was now fully alert. "Was it Leo? Did they catch him?"

"That's what we have to find out. So get yourself out of that bed. You and I have an appointment with the chief."

Half an hour later, Tom's van arrived at Jefferson High, just as an ambulance pulled away from the school and turned toward Central Hills Hospital. The area in front of the auditorium was floodlit, with several police officers poking around the parking lot and surrounding lawns. Chief of Police Robin Montague was directing the operation.

"Chief Montague! What's going on?"

She turned. "Hello, Tom. Hi, Sandra. Glad you came."

"Who was in the ambulance?" Sandra asked.

"Sergeant Abel Driese. A good officer. He got creamed as he tried to stop Captain Invisible."

"What happened?" Tom asked.

"I was playing a long shot," said Chief Montague. "I thought it just possible that this Captain Invisible might return here before the displays were dismantled. So I set up an appropriate reception."

Sandra looked around at all the activity. "Why did you think he would come back?"

"Because this is where he got the bike and the fire suit. If he was greedy enough, it seemed to me he might want more."

"Makes sense," Tom agreed. "So what went wrong?"

"Everything. Because I wanted to catch him in the act, I held my people back as he entered the school through a service tunnel.

As expected, he came out through the loading doors and headed for the jet cycle. That was when we turned on the lights and ordered him to surrender.''

Robin Montague took a deep breath. "I was careless. To avoid them being detected, I located my people too far back. It gave the elusive captain enough time to get Tom's machine into the air—and in the process, sent Abel to the hospital.''

"Captain Invisible was wearing my suit?" Sandra asked.

"The whole time."

Tom looked closely at Chief Montague. "There's more, isn't there?"

She chuckled dryly. "Yes, there's more. You see, when that"—her face twisted—"individual came out from the display area, he was empty-handed. So why did he bother? What was the point?"

"Perhaps there was nothing he wanted," Sandra suggested.

"Sandra, put yourself in Captain Invisible's shoes. If you had gone to all that trouble to break into a room filled with items designed and built by some of the finest young minds in the country, wouldn't you at least leave with *something?* In money alone, what's in that display hall must be worth thousands.''

Tom thought about the funds that had been expended on the jet cycle. "And then some," he admitted.

They were just entering the auditorium when one of the police officers came running over. "Chief!"

Robin turned. "What is it, Harris?"

"I was quite close when Captain Invisible collided with Abel. I heard the captain shout something just before that machine speeded up and he got away."

"What did he shout?"

"It was muffled because of the hood he was wearing. But I swear it was something like 'I'm sorry. Didn't mean it.' "

Chief Montague's eyebrows shot up. "He apologized?"

"That's right, Chief. And it sounded like he meant it."

Tom's thoughts were racing. "Captain Invisible didn't act like a criminal when he came to the aid of those old people. So maybe he isn't a criminal at all. Perhaps what happened to that police officer was just an accident. It would explain his attempt to apologize."

The chief asked, "Harris, did he say anything else?"

"Not that I heard. But this might be important—he stammers."

Tom and Sandra looked at each other. Tom moved his head subtly from side to side. Sandra knew he meant for her not to say anything. They were both aware that Leo tended to stutter when he was excited. But Tom wasn't ready to give Leo's name to the police. He wanted to find Leo first. Or if he couldn't, he at least wanted some hard evidence that Leo was involved before he accused his classmate of theft and other crimes.

"I need your expertise, Chief Montague said. "Although Captain Invisible may not have taken anything with him, it's quite possible he removed items and then stashed them somewhere around here so he could return and retrieve them later. I want you to check the displays."

"That could take hours," Tom pointed out. "Sandra and I have barely had a couple of hours' sleep."

"I'm only asking for a cursory examination. My own people will do a detailed inventory later. Meanwhile, a glance by a knowledgeable eye might reveal a lot more than a detailed examination by a group of nonprofessionals."

Tom and Sandra separated and began to walk the aisles between and around the displays. About half an hour later, when Tom glimpsed Sandra along a cross aisle, she beckoned him over.

Sandra was standing by Leo's exhibit. "Tom, when I walked over here, I found Leo's computer on. It seems to be the only piece of equipment that was touched. I think it proves that Leo is the mysterious Captain Invisible."

"That's only circumstantial evidence, Sandra. Anyone could have turned it on. But I agree with you. It does seem to point to Leo."

"But why would he have come back here, Tom? You don't really think he was planning to steal more of the exhibits, do you?"

"No. I don't know what he thinks he's doing as Captain Invisible, but I can't believe that Leo has turned into a criminal. In fact, I think it's just the opposite. I think Leo finally came to his senses. He wasn't looking to steal anything, Sandra. I'll bet that Captain Invisible came here to return our inventions and was stopped by the police before he could do it."

Tom and Sandra reported to Chief Montague that nothing else appeared to be missing. They didn't mention Leo's computer. By the time they returned home, dawn was just beginning to lighten the eastern horizon.

"I'm exhausted," Sandra said.

"Me, too. But I've got too much buzzing around my brain to sleep now. I'm going down to the lab."

"What for?" Sandra asked.

"I've got an idea of how I can trace the jet bike. If it works, it will either prove that Leo is Captain Invisible, or that he's not involved with all of the nonsense that's been going on."

Sandra nodded. "I'll join you."

Tom gave her a quizzical look.

"I have to run more tests on the buckycloth, Tom. I won't be able to sleep until I know everything there is to know about my surprising invention."

By nine o'clock, Tom and Sandra were eating breakfast together.

"How'd your tests go?" Tom asked.

Sandra frowned and said, "Better than I had expected. My little invention has all sorts of interesting properties. And dangerous ones, too."

Tom could see that Sandra was reluctant to speak, so he urged her on.

"Above a critical temperature level, the material stores kinetic thermal energy," she continued. "The buckycloth not only deflects fire, it's actually able to absorb some of the fire's heat energy. Initially this doesn't have any effect on the wearer. But once the stored energy reaches a critical level, the buckycloth tends to release it in bursts. And the cloth releases the energy inwardly. The person wearing the cloth would feel a burst of energy like a shot of adrenaline. That would explain how you sprinted to the infirmary like Carl Lewis while you were carrying me. But if the energy surge is large enough, it can overload the cardiovascular system of the wearer. In other words, it can cause the wearer to have a heart attack."

Tom munched thoughtfully on a roll before saying anything. He could see how upset Sandra was about the unexpectedly deadly aspect of her fire suit. Finally he said, "Don't blame yourself. The suit is a prototype. You never meant for it to be worn in dangerous situations until it was thoroughly tested. This just means that we've got to find Leo as soon as possible. And I think my little gadget here can help us do that."

"Say, got any more rolls?" Rick Cantwell asked as he sauntered into the breakfast room. He had come to drive Tom and Sandra to school.

"Sure, help yourself, Rick," Sandra said.

Turning back to Tom, she asked, "And exactly what is this new invention of yours?"

Tom held up a device that looked like a hand calculator with a small funnel at one end. "It's a detector,' he said.

"What's it supposed to detect?" Rick asked between mouthfuls.

"It will detect residues from the special-formula fuel in my jet cycle. A tiny fan draws air in through the funnel end. An analyzer searches for telltale traces of the fuel, and the results are displayed on the small screen at the back."

Sandra was up in a flash. "Great, Tom. We can go past Leo's house on the way to school, and you can snoop around with it."

"Sniff around is more like it," said Rick with a grin. "Say! That's a great name for it: Tom Swift's Electronic Sniffer. What do you think, Tom? Tom?"

But Tom and Sandra were already heading for the door. Over her shoulder Sandra called, "Rick! Stop stuffing your face and let's go!"

Then, in a quiet voice she said to Tom, "We've got to find Leo before my suit kills him."

10

CAPTAIN INVISIBLE, ALIAS LEO CAMPBELL, had been out riding over the desert for hours. Everything had gone wrong. He hadn't been able to return the stolen inventions. The police had been waiting for him, and he had probably seriously injured one of them.

Leo felt terrible about it all. There was only one thing left for him to do. He decided to fly the jet cycle out to Swift Enterprises and confront Tom and Sandra. He would tell them the whole story and take whatever was coming to him.

"It's the right thing to do," Leo said out loud. He began to feel better.

As he flew back to Central Hills, he crossed over the seedy side of town. Hawking's Flats was notorious as a hangout for criminals and other lowlife types.

Suddenly Leo heard a woman scream. He was over and past the spot before the sound had registered. Maybe I should go see if someone needs help, he thought. It's another chance for me to do some good before I give myself up. I'll do it!

Leo turned the jet cycle around and swooped back to the place where he'd heard the scream. Sure enough, three street thugs had mugged a young woman and were playing catch with her handbag while they shoved her around.

"Here, Mikey—catch!" said the largest of the three. He had a greasy beard and dirty-looking red hair. He wore a T-shirt that had *Commandos* written in red on it. He tossed the bag high in the air.

Mikey reached up to catch the bag but instead got knocked flat on his back by an invisible fist. The bag, as though it had suddenly sprouted wings, bobbed up and down in the air and began to move around the other two thugs.

"Let's get out of here!" yelled the big one. The third punk pushed the woman to the ground and ran for his life. Bewildered, the woman looked up. There was her bag being held by a man in a mirrored suit, with a strange-looking mask and goggles.

She gasped. "Oh, my—you must be Captain Invisible."

Behind the mask, Leo smiled. He helped the woman up. This is what it feels like to be a real superhero, he thought.

"Yes, madam," he said in as deep a voice as he could muster. "I am Captain Invisible. Dedicated to helping innocent victims of the crime and misery that are part of modern life."

The woman smiled at him. Leo was pleased that he had correctly remembered Stargo Hawk's speech from the comic book's very first issue. Then Leo realized that this was real life, not a comic book.

"Actually," he began, "it's really Tom Swift—"

But the woman was no longer smiling at him. Her eyes went wide, and she screamed, "Look out! Behind you!"

It was the next-to-last thing Leo heard before he blacked out. The last thing he heard was the dull thud of a two-by-four hitting the back of his masked head.

"Let's take my van and leave your Jaguar here, Rick," said Tom. "I don't want to call a whole lot of attention to our snooping around.''

They piled into the van, and Rick stumbled over a pile of what felt like steel bars.

As he was picking himself up, he heard a voice say, ''I told you I should have been given retractable legs, Tom.''

''Yes, Rob, I know. It's on my list,'' said Tom. ''But for the time being, try to squeeze out of the way as much as possible.''

The seven-foot-tall gleaming metal robot tried to obey. But after almost smacking Sandra in the head with a steel elbow, Tom told him, ''Rob! Just be still. Rick will climb over you, and Sandra can sit on you.''

Once they were settled, Sandra said, ''Why are we bringing Rob, Tom?''

''My little sniffer, as Rick called it, will only pick up strong signals, say an hour old. But Rob has equipment that is much more sophisticated. If I don't find anything with the sniffer, we'll see how well Rob can do.''

''Actually, Tom, you needn't have bothered cobbling together your little odor-eating device at all. My sensors can easily pick up the hydrocarbon residue left by the jet bike exhaust, even after some time and at a considerable distance."

Tom turned his head slightly and stared at the giant robot. "Rob, I lost six hours of sleep cobbling that little thing together. Why didn't you tell me?"

"Because, Tom, you have always instructed me that you are not to be disturbed when you are in your lab, cobbling."

Tom sighed. "At least we'll be able to do this faster than I thought. Rick, you won't have to miss first-period math," he said.

Rick's eyes widened. He glared at the gleaming photocells in Rob's eye sockets. "Thanks a heap, big guy!"

"You are welcome, Rick," said the robot.

When they arrived at Leo's house, Tom said, "Look. The garage door's open, and Leo's pickup truck is gone. He must be on his way to school."

Tom pulled halfway up the driveway and stopped the van. "Sandra, please open the rear door," he said. "Now, Rob, sniff."

The metal giant leaned toward the open van door. "I have it, Tom," he said quietly. "The jet cycle was here less than twenty-four hours ago."

"What now?" asked Rick.

"Now you close the door and we go to school," Tom said with a grin.

As they drove, Tom put on the radio. There was a newscast in progress.

". . . Mrs. Daley was mugged on the way to her job as a nurse in Hawking's Clinic. The mysterious superpowered individual who calls himself Captain Invisible not only chased off the muggers and saved her handbag—which, she revealed, held checks totaling a thousand dollars that she would later deposit at her bank—he told Mrs. Daley his real name. Of course, the connection had been there all along, said police detective Emile Karvetti. It was he who first identified the description of Captain Invisible's flying machine and his costume as matching the stolen inventions of Tom Swift and his sister, Sandra.

"Detective Karvetti said he was not surprised that the mystery man was Tom Swift all along. Still, Police Chief Robin Montague said that no official identification had been made. And given the teenage inventor's sterling reputation in the community—"

"Tom! What's going on?" asked Rick.

"Quiet!" Tom said, with a quick wave of his hand. "There's more. Listen."

". . . Mrs. Daley said that after the fallen thug had gotten back up and whacked Captain Invisible with a broken two-by-four, she ran for her life. But when she was half a block away, she turned around to see if she was being followed. She says that she saw the other two thugs return in a pickup truck. They threw the limp body of the costumed vigilante in the back and put his vehicle in there as well."

Tom slammed on the brakes and made a quick U-turn. Sandra was thrown to the floor, and Rick almost fell out of his seat.

As she was picking herself back up, Sandra asked, "Where are we going?"

"Back home," said Tom. "We weren't there when Mom and Dad woke up. If they've heard that news broadcast, who knows what they'll think has happened."

Sandra and Rick exchanged a fast glance. "Step on it!" they said at the same time.

Rob calculated exactly when the lights would change, allowing Tom to go the limit without hardly braking. They made it home in record time.

"Tom! Thank heavens you're okay," said his mother as he burst in through the door.

Mr. Swift went over to Tom, smiled at him, and gave him a friendly bear hug. "I knew you weren't mixed up in it," he said. "But where were you?"

Tom explained what he'd been up to.

"But where are Sandra and Rick now?" asked Mr. Swift.

"Sandra took Rob back to the lab, and then Rick took her to school in his Jaguar. Poor Rick. It looks like he's going to miss his first class, after all," Tom said with a mischievous grin.

"Mikey, I can't believe it! We bagged Tom Swift and two of his super-duper inventions." The redheaded thug, whose name was Chris, chuckled and shook his head in wonder.

"The only problem now is, what are we going to do with them?"

"Easy," said Chris. "We'll take 'em to Jocko's. I bet he'll pay us plenty, too."

"Say, that's right!" said Mikey. "Jocko handles stolen cars, and motorcycles, too."

"Ha! He handles more than that, kid," said Chris. "Jocko's got his finger in every sweet deal going on in this city. He fences stolen gems and jewelry, sells the best guns—he has the toughest mob I've ever seen."

"And now he's going to have Tom Swift and his invisible suit. I know how he can use the suit and the flying motorcycle. But what do you think he'll do with Swift?"

"Who cares?" said Chris. "Hey—here we are now. Pull around the back."

Jocko Morgan's Antiques Emporium was a legitimate front for a lot of seedy business. Morgan was a big man with a thick fringe of white hair like a halo around his balding head. He wore a diamond pinky ring that looked too big to be real, but it was.

"What have you got for me today, boys?" Jocko asked as he walked into the back room of the store.

Mikey and Chris just stood there grinning. Then Mikey spoke up. "Did you hear the news today, boss?"

Jocko was used to dealing with the limited mental capacity of his two thugs and didn't lose his patience. "Yes, I did," he said. "Now tell me what it has to do with you—and my business."

"We got him, boss," Chris said. "Tom Swift. We nabbed him—and his flying motorcycle, too."

They went out back, to the pickup truck. Chris and Mikey dragged the still unconscious body of Leo Campbell from beneath a plastic sheet. The jet cycle was there next to him.

Jocko Morgan's beady eyes opened wide. "Good work, boys! There'll be an extra bonus in this for you. This guy's worth millions!"

"Millions?" said Chris. "How are we going to get it?"

"Simple," said Jocko. "We hold Tom Swift for ransom."

11

THE RANSOM CALL WAS MADE FROM A PAY phone.

"Thomas Swift, Sr.?"

"Yes. Who is this?"

"I'm the guy that's got your son. Listen close, and listen fast. This only gets said once. Five million, small bills. I call tomorrow to tell you where to deliver it. You get Junior at the same time."

There was a click and then a dial tone. Mr. Swift hung up. "That was them," he said to the other people in the room. Mrs. Swift, Tom, Sandra, Rick, Chief of Police Robin Montague, and Detective Emile Karvetti were there.

"Didn't take them long, did it?" Karvetti said. "That planted news story is only a couple of hours old."

Turning to Tom, he said, "Sorry about the way I popped off at you earlier, kid. But you have to admit, you were the logical suspect."

Tom stuck out his hand, and Karvetti shook it with a smile. "No hard feelings," Tom said. "Now the *kidnappers* think I'm Captain Invisible. At least, whoever's wearing Sandra's suit is now worth keeping alive to them."

"And you have a pretty good idea of just who that is, don't you, Tom?" said Mr. Swift. "I think it's time you told us all."

Tom looked at Sandra. She shrugged and nodded. Tom told them about the fuel residue that he had found in Leo's garage, and Sandra filled in the rest.

"And the worst part is, the suit could kill him at any time," she concluded.

"No," said Tom slowly, "I don't think that's the worst part of it, Sandra." All heads turned toward him.

"I've just been monitoring the news, via audio linkup with Megatron," Tom said, pointing to a small device in his left ear. "The afternoon edition of the Central Hills *Clarion* has my picture along with the story.

When the kidnappers see it, they'll know they haven't got Tom Swift, and Leo's life might not be worth five cents.''

Chief Montague looked hard at Detective Karvetti. "What was the point of asking them to run the story, Emile, if you didn't tell them not to run his picture?" she asked sharply.

Karvetti turned bright red. "Sorry, Chief," he said with a massive shrug of his shoulders. "But it never occurred to me that they'd have it." Turning to the Swifts, he added, "Listen, folks. You have to remember that I'm new in town."

Sandra took a step toward him, but before she got any farther or said anything, Tom stepped in between. "Okay. This just means that we have to find them faster. I'll have one of my techs run Rob around town in the van. We'll find them." He put a hand around Sandra's shoulder and said quietly, "Leo will be all right, you'll see."

Sandra gave Tom a weak smile. Then her jaw firmed up, her lips tightened, and she said, "Right. Well, if you'll excuse us now, Tom and I have some work to do."

"Tom, I think I've got it!" Sandra said as she ran into her brother's lab early the following morning. "I've been working on a simple device to ground the fire suit—take the built-up kinetic thermal charge out of the buckycloth without harming the wearer." She held up what looked like a miniature fishing pole with a metal line attached.

Tom looked up from what he was doing. "That's great, sis. But I'm afraid we're not having as much success as you. Rob has covered half the city in the past twenty-four hours and hasn't picked up the jet cycle's scent. The trail must be too cold." He saw the look in Sandra's eyes and added, "I know. I hope Leo's okay, too. We'll find him soon. If only the kidnappers would use the jet cycle, we could track them down."

At that moment, Tom's intercom buzzed. It was his father.

"Tom, have you heard the morning news yet?"

"No. Why, Dad?"

"Because," Mr. Swift said, "Captain Invisible was seen again last night. Only this time he wasn't helping innocent victims—he was robbing a jewelry store on Almont Street, in Hawking's Flats."

"Thanks for the tip, Dad," Tom said. The intercom clicked off, and Tom turned to Sandra. "Let's check this out. You come too, Rob."

Tom, his sister, and his gleaming robot headed for his van and drove to the scene of the crime.

"I would have covered this area by three this afternoon, Tom," Rob said.

"I know," Tom replied. "We've just saved six hours."

"I still can't believe that Leo would rob a jewelry store," said Sandra. "Besides, how did he get away from the kidnappers?"

"I don't think he did," said Tom. "I think they realized that they didn't have me and came up with another way of making some fast money. And Captain Invisible gets all the blame."

"Then where's Leo?" Sandra asked.

Tom looked grimly ahead. He wanted to give Sandra hope, but there was nothing he could say.

Leo had been roughed up by Jocko Morgan's henchmen before he was even asked a question. "It usually saves so much time," Morgan said as Leo was lifted to his feet. "Now tell me all about Tom Swift and Swift Enterprises."

But Leo had caused enough damage in the past few days and would not talk.

Morgan tried to threaten and bully Leo into telling him all about the layout of Swift

Enterprises—where they kept the computer chips, where they housed their robots, what the security setup was like.

Through his pain, Leo realized that Morgan had mistakenly assumed he was a close friend of Tom's and Sandra's. He smiled bravely and finally said, "I know what you're after, and I know how to get it. But you'll never get the information out of me."

Morgan sighed and motioned to the big man, Chris, who stood behind Leo. Chris took out a sap and smacked Leo across the back of the head. Leo moaned once and fell to the floor, unconscious.

"You want me to make him disappear permanent like, boss?" asked Chris.

But Jocko was a patient man. "No," he said. "We have time. I'm sure our brave friend here can eventually be persuaded to talk. After all, the stakes have gone up. If we can knock over Swift Enterprises, the haul could be worth *billions*."

Tom was frustrated. "Rob, are you sure you can't trace the jet bike's residue through the air?" he asked his gleaming companion.

"Sorry, Tom," said the robot. "But there's too much auto pollution. The hydrocarbon residues all blend together."

Sandra was deeply disappointed. "We might as well go home, Tom," she said. "It doesn't do us any good to know that the jet cycle took off in an easterly direction."

"You're right, Sis," Tom said as he got back into his van. "I've got to think of something else. In the meantime, we'll drop Rob off and then go on to school."

That night, another store was held up by Captain Invisible. This time it was Edmund's Diamond Exchange, just outside of the Hawking's Flats area.

At breakfast the next morning, Sandra was frantic. "Tom, it's been two days. Leo's probably dead by now, and thieves are using our inventions to go on a crime spree. Have you come up with any new ideas yet?"

In fact, Tom had just decided on a new direction for their search. "I think that instead of trying to track down the jet cycle, we've got to track down the thieves themselves."

Sandra was interested. "And how do we go about doing that?" she asked.

Tom put down his napkin, finished his coffee, and said, "Come with me." Then he pulled out his pocket communicator and spoke into it. "Rob, meet us in my lab, please."

Tom and his sister headed for the lab at a sprint. "I should have thought of this before," Tom told Sandra as they entered. He had asked Rob to print out a grid map of the city that centered on Hawking's Flats and the surrounding neighborhoods. Then he'd marked the place where the woman had reported being saved by Captain Invisible, and the two stores that were robbed.

"You see, they're all in the same area."

"Yes," said Sandra. "I see. But why?"

Despite the seriousness of the situation, Tom had to laugh.

"Because the jet cycle needs special fuel. All you have to do is screw the lid off the gas tank and take a whiff. It doesn't smell like any conventional fuel that's available. The crooks are using it up with each crime, so they would want to make optimum use of the jet cycle before the fuel is completely gone. And the way to do that is to commit crimes that are close to your base of operations."

Sandra nodded slowly. "I always said you were a lot smarter than you looked," she said with a straight face. When Tom looked insulted, though, she cracked up.

Laughing helped ease the tension. A minute later, Rob said, "Tom, I've done as you asked. Here are the three most likely places for Captain Invisible to strike next."

Tom looked at the map. "Fine," he said. "Consult with Megatron and see if you can give me the store with the highest probability of being the next target. When Captain Invisible appears tonight," he added grimly, "I want to throw him a surprise party."

"Tom, don't you think you should consult with Chief Montague about this?" Sandra asked. "I mean, after all, you're not a private detective or anything. And this is a police matter."

Tom smiled. "You don't have to worry about my safety, Sis. Rob will be with me. Besides, I think that the police computers are big enough to arrive at the same conclusions that we do."

"Of course," said Sandra. "Just make sure that you don't screw up a police stakeout, or Chief Montague will skin you alive."

Tom laughed. But inside he was thinking, I wonder how that would compare with what Leo might be going through right now?

LEO CAMPBELL WAS PLAYING FOR TIME. HE
hadn't been conscious for more than a few
hours the past two days and had sustained
brutal beatings when he was. Still, he realized that he was fortunate to be alive.

Just then he was writing a list of totally
false codes and passwords for Swift Enterprises, as his personal tormentor Chris
stood watch over him.

I'll give them some of what they want,
Leo thought. Then I'll tell them that my
brains are so scrambled from my being
knocked about that I'm having a hard time
remembering the rest. That should give me
another day or two. And then what? Leo

sent a silent prayer that Tom and Sandra Swift would be able to find him before Jocko Morgan finally lost his patience.

Leo figured that the Swifts, and probably the police as well, must be looking for their inventions. In the past, Leo might have tried to imagine what Stargo Hawk would do in a situation like this. By now, though, the reality of what being a superhero was all about had been made quite clear to Leo. It was much different from the fantasy, and Leo couldn't quite believe he had ever been so dumb as to try acting like a comic book vigilante. He knew that his only hope now was to stall—and pray for help.

"Let's go over the list again, Rob," said Tom Swift. They were in his lab, looking at the locations of the stores that Rob and Megatron had picked as being Captain Invisible's most likely targets.

Two places had been given equal probability: a jewelry store on East Lompas, and a small commercial bank five blocks away from it. Captain Invisible had already robbed two jewelry stores, and Rob thought that established a clear enough pattern to make Walken's Jewelry Store the next logical target.

Tom went to his computer and opened a

dialogue with Megatron. "Factoring in what you know about human tendencies, do you agree that Walken's is the right choice?" he typed in.

"Logically, Tom, it should be," Megatron responded. "But factoring in the illogical behavior of humans, I'd say that the bank will be the next target."

"So we will be watching the bank tonight, Tom?" asked Rob.

Tom turned to the gleaming robot and smiled. "No, Rob. We'll watch the jewelry store."

"But you just read Megatron's opinion. And I have found the Megatron system to be one hundred percent accurate when I am working with it on one of your new inventions."

"Yes, Rob. The system is accurate— when human quirks are not involved. Since the bank is the logical choice, and since many human decisions defy logic, I'll play my hunch on the jewelry store."

Rob's photocell receptors glowed deep orange, always an indication that he was involved in serious calculation. "If I follow your line of reasoning, Tom, I will become lost in a subetheric paradox loop that will short out all of my circuits and damage my most sensitive chips. Your line of thinking is not only illogical, it is dangerous to robotic health.''

Tom couldn't help but laugh. "Okay, Rob. I order you not to try to figure out the logic of my statements," he finally said.

The fierce glow in Rob's eye sockets softened. "Thank you, Tom," he said. "I will get the van ready for our evening stakeout."

"Keep out of sight until I kill the lights, Rob," said Tom. It was just past midnight as he parked his van across the street from Walken's Jewelry Store, shut off the engine and the lights, and took out a pair of infrared binoculars. Walken's was on the ground floor of a two-story building, flanked on one side by an office tower, and on the other by a parking lot.

"We should be able to get a good view from here of anyone coming or going," Tom said quietly. Rob was now squeezed in beside Tom in the front seat. Tom had his window open, and Rob was alert for any telltale hydrocarbons.

After a few minutes, Rob said, "Your choice may have been right after all, Tom. The jet cycle has definitely been in this area. As recently as yesterday."

Tom nodded and put down his binoculars. All was quiet. He turned on his Walkman and listened to ZZ Top singing about cars and girls and life on the road.

Tom leaned back in his seat and began to settle into a narrow zone between relaxation and alertness. The two robberies occurred between midnight and three A.M., he thought. I can last three hours, no problem. After that, I'll have to get some sleep and put Rob on full alert.

About an hour later, Rob said, "Tom, there are three people on the roof of the office tower. Two other people are concealed within doorways farther down the street. I would say that they have been here for approximately ten minutes."

Now fully awake and focused, Tom said, "What are they doing, Rob?"

"They are watching," said his metallic companion.

"Anything else?" Tom asked. He now had his binoculars trained on the roof of the office building. Sure enough, he could make out the humped backs of three people crouched by the roof's edge.

"Tom, they are all carrying weapons."

A sudden thought occurred to Tom. "Can you identify any of them, Rob?"

"Yes, Tom. Police Chief Robin Montague is hiding in the second doorway to the left of the jewelry store."

Tom sighed and relaxed. Just as I thought. Their computers must have popped up the same list as Rob and Megatron had. Well, at least I know I'm in good company.

"Rob, I think I'll try to get some sleep now. Wake me as soon as you see any suspicious movement—either among those watching or on the street itself."

It was four A.M. when Rob gently nudged Tom into wakefulness. It took Tom a few moments to get his bearings. Then he asked, "What's up, Rob?" as he stifled a yawn.

"The watchers have all abandoned their posts, Tom."

"Can you see where they've gone?"

"They have left the area, Tom," Rob responded.

Tom looked at his watch and understood why. "We're going, too, Rob," he said. "Looks like my hunch was wrong, after all."

"In that case, Tom," said the robot, "so was the police's."

Tom smiled at Rob. He knew his gleaming companion was trying to make him feel better. "Thanks, Rob," he said. Then he started the van and said, "Let's go home. I can still get a few hours' sleep before my first class."

But at seven A.M. Sandra was in his room shaking him awake.

"Tom—come on, Tom. Wake up!"

"Huh? What happened?" he asked as he reached groggily for his bathrobe.

"Here. Listen to this." Sandra played back a tape for him. "It was broadcast on the news a couple of minutes ago. I got most of it on tape."

". . . Although the bank has yet to do a final check, it is estimated that approximately one hundred thousand dollars was stolen from the night deposit vault.

"Witnesses report seeing a flying vehicle entering and leaving the area. No rider was seen on it, however, leading the police to conclude that Captain Invisible has struck again."

Tom groaned and held his head in his hands. He gave Sandra a sheepish look through his fingers, then sat up and stretched the kinks out of his joints. He told Sandra about his stakeout.

Sandra laughed when he was done. "Well, don't tell Rob. There'll be no living with him if he thinks that he knows human psychology better than we do."

That night Tom and Rob were back at the jewelry store. Rob had insisted that it was now the most logical next target, and Tom had agreed.

It was just past midnight when Rob said quietly, "Jet cycle approaching, Tom. Low and fast." Rob pointed through the open window.

Tom's heart thumped wildly as he focused his binoculars in the indicated direction. Sure enough, there was the telltale faint glow of twin jet exhausts as his cycle slid down from the sky and disappeared behind the building that housed the jewelry store.

A minute later, Tom and Rob watched as a figure dressed in Sandra's fire suit crept around the corner and removed a miniature acetylene torch from a bag on his shoulder.

It took only five minutes for the fire-suited figure to cut through the metal gates covering the store's display windows.

Even with his infrared binoculars, Tom couldn't quite make out what the figure was doing next. "Rob, what's happening now?" he asked.

"The person has now removed what appears to be a long-handled glass cutter and several tiny suction cups from the bag, Tom."

Tom nodded as he noted the professional ease with which Captain Invisible removed a large section of glass, lifted it clear, and then laid it gently on the sidewalk. Stepping in through the opening, the captain disappeared inside the store.

"Okay, Rob," said Tom. "Let's go." Quickly and quietly they left the van and, staying low, hurried across the street.

Peering through the now empty window space, Tom could see that the thief had already emptied the interior display cases and was busily working on a safe in the rear of the store.

Tom calmly removed a thin device from his pocket. It was a high-intensity flashlight, capable of throwing a wide beam of blinding light. He turned it on the thief, and whispered, "Now, Rob!"

Caught in the intense beam, the thief suddenly straightened up and turned to look for its source. At that moment, Rob said: "You are surrounded! Come out slowly with your hands above your head!" Rob's metallic voice sounded just as though it had come through a police bullhorn.

Blinded by the light, Captain Invisible raised his hands and began stumbling his way to the front of the store.

Tom and Rob climbed through the window space into the store. But in the process,

Tom could not hold the beam steadily on the criminal's face.

No longer blinded, he now saw what was coming at him. "Hey!" he yelled. "You're not the cops!" He quickly ducked down out of sight.

Tom went to take another step and found himself looking at the floor. Rob had knocked him down—just a microsecond before a bullet whizzed through the space where Tom had been standing. The thief had a handgun with a silencer attached!

Quickly Tom found the flashlight again and played it on the thief's masked face. Captain Invisible put a hand up to block out the light and began shooting again. He couldn't see clearly, but Rob's silhouette was a big target.

Tom crouched and counted. Five, six, seven shots. And then a distant click. "That's it, Rob," he whispered to the still-standing giant. "He's out of ammo." Tom stood up again, and said, "Charge him!"

But before the robot could act, he first checked to make sure that Tom was safe. In that moment's time, Captain Invisible took an object from a belt around his waist and threw it with all his might.

With electronic speed, Rob caught the missile in midair. The firebomb exploded on contact and burst into flame. Within moments, Tom was surrounded by a raging inferno. He could no longer see the thief, nor Rob—nor any way out of the store before he and it were consumed by the rapidly spreading flames.

TOM SWIFT INSTINCTIVELY PUT HIS HANDS
in front of his face and stumbled backward,
away from the flames.

Moving with a blur of speed, Rob picked
up a six-foot-long wooden countertop and
threw it past Tom's ear. It landing with un-
erring accuracy—one end on the floor, the
other sticking out through the empty window space.

"Quick, Tom," called the robot. "Take
two steps back, and you'll be on the ramp."
Blinded by smoke and flames, Tom groped
his way back to the improvised ramp and
managed to crawl up it and out of the store.

Once outside, Tom stumbled a few steps

and fell to his knees, trying to clear his eyes and lungs. After two deep breaths, he was able to call out, "Rob! Can you see if the thief is still in the store?"

A split second later, Rob was by his side, helping Tom up. "He went out the back way, Tom," said Rob, his once-gleaming exterior now covered with smoky soot.

"The jet cycle!" Tom said. "Quick, Rob, stop him before he can power up and take off!"

The robot accelerated with incredible speed, heading for the back alley. Tom staggered along behind him. By the time he reached the alley, Rob was in the process of pulling Captain Invisible off the jet cycle.

But the thief managed to struggle free and tried to run past Rob. In a moment, he had blurred into invisibility. Tom was stunned. He had never seen the fire suit's invisibility effect in action. Then he saw something even more astounding.

Rob's hand shot out to stop the thief, but then the giant robot rose into the air, lifted by unseen hands. The suit must have released a burst of thermal energy that it absorbed from the fire, Tom realized, giving the thief superhuman strength.

The fight between Rob and the invisible criminal took place at lightning speed. Tom

couldn't tell exactly what was happening—
or who was getting the better and the worse
of it.

Then, as quickly as it had begun, the fight
was over, and Rob was looming above the
still figure of Captain Invisible. Tom walked
over. The thief was definitely down for the
count. There was no movement from him at
all.

Although moments before Tom had been
rooting for Rob to beat the thief's brains in,
he was now concerned. He quickly removed
the thief's breathing mask and goggles, and
unfastened the front of the fire suit. He
placed his ear next to the man's nose but
couldn't hear any sound of breathing. Nor
could he find more than a very weak pulse
on the man's neck. He quickly stripped the
rest of the suit from the unconscious figure.

"Rob," he said, "this man's in cardiac
arrest. Give him CPR, and then take him to
the Hawking's Flats hospital in my van."
As he spoke, Tom began to put on the fire
suit.

He was dressed in seconds, and then
knelt next to Rob as the gentle giant adminis-
tered cardiopulmonary resuscitation.

"His heart has started again, Tom, although it is quite weak," Rob reported.

Tom heaved a sigh of relief. Sandra had

invented the fire suit to save lives, not take them. Bending closer, Tom quickly went through the man's pockets. They were empty, except for a book of matches bearing the legend Morgan's Antiques Emporium, with an address below the name.

"Bingo," said Tom. He finished placing the breathing mask and goggles over his face and hopped on the jet cycle. He checked the fuel gauge. It was almost empty, as Tom knew it had to be. Then he got off the flying machine and headed back into the still-blazing jewelry store. The flames didn't bother him at all as he reached through them to pick up some of the items the thief had intended to steal.

Tom started the cycle and slowly rode it over to the van. Rob had already placed the criminal's unmoving body in the back. Tom reached carefully around it and came up with a sack similar to the one the thief had been carrying. As he placed the jewelry in it, he said, "Rob, take careful note of the items I'm borrowing. I want to make sure everything gets returned when this is all over."

"Tom," said Rob, "I see what you have in mind. But I can't allow you to wear that suit. It could cause you the same kind of damage it's done to this man."

"It's okay, Rob," said Tom. "He's suffering from a massive spontaneous release of thermal energy from the suit. There's probably not enough left in it now for more than a small jolt."

Rob didn't move. He stood stock-still, his photoreceptors shining with a deep orange glow.

"I'll be fine, Rob," Tom reassured him. "Now, here's the plan. First, call the fire department. Then, after you take the man to the hospital, call Dad. Tell him that if I don't get back home within the hour, he should call Chief Montague and have her come to Morgan's Antiques Emporium on East Street."

"Is that where you'll be, Tom?" asked Rob.

Tom nodded. "And, with any luck, that's where Leo Campbell will be, too."

Without saying another word, Tom powered up the jet cycle and took off down the street. Within fifty feet he was airborne and rising fast.

"Good luck, Tom!" Rob called from the street below to the quickly disappearing figure.

I'll need it, Tom thought as he leaned into the wind.

Morgan's Emporium was only a half mile

away. A good thing, Tom thought as he looked again at the fuel gauge. The indicator was well into the red now, meaning that the cycle was running on its emergency fuel supply.

A few seconds later, Tom began his descent. He spotted Morgan's. It was the only store on the block with a light on. Tom slowed the cycle and landed it in the alley behind the store. Clearly Captain Invisible could not be seen entering the store through the front door, Tom figured, so there must be a back entrance. Sure enough, there was.

Tom found a large tarpaulin and threw it over the jet cycle. Then, taking a deep breath to calm his nerves, he turned the handle on the back door and walked into the store.

Inside, he almost bumped into the burly figure of Morgan's goon Mikey. "Hey, Butch! You're back early, aren't you?" the thug said.

Tom raised the bag and pointed at it. Then he shook it for emphasis.

Mikey smiled at the sound of jingling jewelry. "Say, Jocko's going to like this," he said, clapping Tom on the back. "A good haul—and fast, too."

As they walked into the dimly lit back room, Mikey said, "Jocko's upstairs with the jerk now. He's going to give him one last chance to supply the security codes. If he don't get them tonight, Chris is finally going to be allowed to tear that guy into little pieces. And then tear the pieces into smaller pieces," he added with a nasty chuckle. "Go on up. I'm sure Jocko'll be glad to see you—and the goodies you brought him." He laughed again.

Behind his mask, Tom gave as nasty a chuckle as he could, and said, "Right!"

But as he started to climb the stairs, Tom felt himself getting light-headed. He was having trouble breathing. He realized what was happening and broke out in a cold sweat.

The suit's air supply is almost out! he thought. I was so concerned about the jet cycle, I forgot all about the way the fire suit works. It has a self-contained air supply, so that the wearer doesn't have to worry about breathing superheated air in a fire.

Halfway up the stairs, Tom opened the neck ring of the suit and unfastened it at the top. It let in a trickle of air. He took a couple of deep breaths, and his head began to clear. Just then he heard a scream from somewhere above him. It's Leo! he thought, and raced up the rest of the way.

He ran to the door to the room that the screams had come from. Forcing himself to be calm, he turned the handle and walked in.

Tom scanned the room with a quick glance. There was an old wood-burning fireplace, with a nice fire going in it. There was an old, soiled mattress on the floor, a rickety wooden table, and two chairs. A balding fat man sat with his back to Tom. Slumping over in the chair across from him was another figure, which Tom guessed had to be Leo, although the man who must be Jocko Morgan blocked his view.

"Hello, Jocko," Tom said as casually as he could.

The big man with the balding head looked up from what he was doing. Then Tom saw Leo. Leo was bleeding from his nose, one of his eyes was swollen shut, and he was moaning.

"Here's tonight's haul," Tom said, holding up the bag. As Morgan reached for it, Tom swung it with all his might and knocked Jocko off his chair. The big man hit the floor with a thud. Tom quickly turned and closed the door.

Leo had collapsed into unconsciousness again. Tom felt as if he was going to pass out himself. Then he heard the rush of footsteps up the stairs as the rest of Morgan's gang came to see what was going on. Tom knelt beside the still body of Morgan and quickly searched his pockets. The door had a keyhole in it, Tom realized. If I can find the key and lock the door, I can buy myself another minute or two.

Tom found the key, but he was having trouble breathing again. He removed the hood of the fire suit completely and stood up. He could breathe fine now, but he was feeling awfully light-headed. Tom staggered over to the door and fumbled the key into the lock. Before he could turn it, the door opened from the other side.

For a timeless moment, Tom and Mikey stared at each other. Then someone behind Mikey shouted, "Hey! That's not Butch!" Tom tried to slam the door shut, but the weight of several bodies on the other side was too great. The door was pushed open, and Tom went flying.

Tom was overmatched by the gang of thieves. A couple of minutes later, he was tied to a chair, back to back with Leo, who was just beginning to come around.

Jocko Morgan had obviously hit his head hard on the floor. There was a small pool of blood underneath him. Morgan's men hovered over him, trying to bring him back to consciousness, with no success.

Chris stepped forward and walked over to

Tom. Tom looked up at the man with fury in his eyes. Chris smiled evilly and smacked Tom in the side of the head with his beefy hand. Tom saw stars. He shook his head to clear it and spat blood.

"You must be crazy, walking in here like this all by yourself," said the thug.

"Chris," said Mikey, "Jocko's still out. What should we do?"

"It's simple. We take Morgan to the doc, load the truck with our loot, get rid of these two, and then scram."

Chris nodded to two of the men, and without saying another word, they lifted up the large body of Jocko Morgan and carried him out of the room.

"Mikey, start loading the truck. I'll take care of these two," Chris said. He pulled a gun from his back pocket and checked to make sure that it was loaded.

He walked around to face Tom and said, "I don't know what you did to Butch, but I'm sure what I'm going to do to you will be much worse." He pointed the gun at Tom and cocked the hammer.

14

TOM SWIFT WAS DESPERATE. HE SEARCHED
the room with his eyes, looking for anything
that might help. There was nothing but the
fire burning in the fireplace.

Fire! Tom thought. I'm still wearing the
suit—it might be my only weapon. But how
can I use it?

"I think I'll shoot your kneecaps first,"
Chris was saying. "They say it's about the
most pain a person can feel without passing
out. And I don't want you to pass out, kid.
You've got to be awake for all the fun."

At that moment, one of the other thugs
came running into the room.

"Chris! Quick—we got to get out of here!
The cops are all over the place!"

Sure enough, through the closed windows in the room they could hear an amplified voice saying, "This is the police. We know you're in there. We have the place surrounded. Come out with your hands above your heads. We have the place—"

It was all the distraction that Tom needed. Although his hands were tied behind him, his legs were free. He braced his back against Leo's, lifted his legs, and swung them at Chris's hands.

The kick caused Chris's gun to jump into the air. With uncanny accuracy, it landed in the fireplace and discharged. The blast had several effects, all at once.

It knocked two logs out of the fire. One of them fell on the mattress, which immediately started to burn. The other log hit one of the thugs squarely in the chest. He screamed and ran from the room, trying to put out the flames.

Shots were fired through the window, and the police began to rush the building.

In moments, the flames took hold in the small room.

"Forget about this!" Chris shouted. "Let's go!"

The thugs ran out, leaving Tom and Leo to face the rising flames.

Tom's mind raced. There's never a superhero around when you really need one, he thought. Wait a second! *I'm* wearing the fire suit now. Tom swung his legs around so that they were directly in the flames of the burning mattress.

My only hope is that the suit will store up some thermal energy and release it quickly, Tom thought. Then I should get a burst of superenergy—and I'm going to need it to get us out of here.

At that moment, Leo came to. He saw the room on fire and realized that he was tied to someone else. Craning his neck around, he saw who it was.

"Tom! How did you get here? What's happening?" Leo mumbled.

"Steady, Leo," Tom said through gritted teeth. "I've got to charge the fire suit, or we'll never get out of here. If I can get closer to the fire, it would help."

Tom and Leo rocked their chairs back and forth, and a few moments later they crashed sideways to the floor. Tom's body was in the midst of the fire—but so was Leo's.

Leo screamed in pain. Tom saw what was happening and flexed his wrists with all his might. The ropes that were holding him tore away like tissue paper. Tom quickly ripped off the ropes that held Leo and scooped him up.

Tom retrieved the fire suit's hood and mask from where they lay on the floor and headed for the door. He swung Leo up and over his shoulder, in a fireman's carry. With his free hand, he gave Leo the hood and mask.

"Put them on," he said. "Take a deep breath and hold it. I'm going to run through the fire and get us out of here!"

Leo did what Tom said. Tom took a deep breath, closed his eyes, and plunged into the fire.

He found the stairs by feel alone and ran down. He didn't stop running until he had carried Leo out of the building and into the street.

It was like a scene from a disaster movie. Police, fire, and emergency vehicles were all over the street. Jocko Morgan was being placed on a stretcher and taken to a waiting ambulance.

Police chief Robin Montague was directing the action through a bullhorn. "Karvetti! Go with Morgan to the hospital. Don't let him out of your sight! Spangler and Matthews, take those other thugs to the wagon and search them thoroughly. Then get them to a lockup, fast!"

Tom stood there, with Leo still over his shoulder, taking it all in. He was dazed but delighted. Then he saw Sandra and his father running toward him.

"Tom! Your face is burned! Are you all right?" asked Mr. Swift as he came close.

"Tom! Is that Leo?" Sandra asked.

Tom realized that he was still holding Leo. He put him down and saw that Leo's arms were burned, but despite the bruises on his face, he appeared to be okay.

Then Sandra and Mr. Swift were at his side. He smiled at them and then promptly passed out. Leo, burned arms and all, caught Tom before he hit the ground.

Mr. Swift wanted Tom to come home, where he could have the finest round-the-clock care. But Tom had insisted on staying in the Hawking's Flats hospital with Leo. The two of them were sharing a room.

Tom wanted to make sure that Leo knew he was all right, and that he wouldn't have to worry about anything while he recovered. Leo was loving it. The fact that Sandra visited them every day probably had something to do with that, Tom figured.

It was the day after Tom had rescued Leo, and they were both well enough to tell the entire story to Chief Montague and Mr. Swift.

"Leo, what you did was wrong. You know that, don't you?" said Robin Montague.

Leo nodded. "I'm willing to accept complete responsibility for my actions, even if I have to go to prison," he said solemnly.

Chief Montague suppressed a smile. "I don't think that will be necessary, Leo. The police officer whom you thought you injured when we surprised you in the school auditorium is fine. He doesn't wish to press charges. The Swifts have informed me that you were *testing* their equipment, with their permission. The people you helped as Captain Invisible never saw your face. And almost all of the jewelry and money stolen by the other Captain Invisible has been recovered. The school authorities have acceded to Mr. Swift's request and will not charge you with theft. And they can't charge you with breaking into the school illegally, because the 'door' you entered through was never kept locked."

Leo heaved a sigh of relief. "Thanks," he said. "And I mean all of you. Tom, Sandra, Mr. Swift, and Chief Montague. I'd like to shake hands with each of you, but"—he nodded at his bandages—"that will have to wait.

"I still can't believe that I could have been that dumb," Leo continued with a shake of his head. "I just never realized how big a difference there is between real life and fantasies. I still love my comics. But I'll never again think of Stargo Hawk as my idol. I can't thank you all enough, for saving my life and bringing me to my senses."

"Yeah—before you did something *really* stupid," said Rick as he walked into the room. He greeted everyone and then walked over to Leo.

"I'm glad I heard you say you still like comics, because these cost me ten bucks," Rick said as he put down a stack of comic books next to Leo's bed.

Before he could say anything else, a nurse walked into the room. "Excuse me, Leo," she said, "but you have another visitor."

All heads turned to watch a well-dressed elderly gentleman walk into the room.

"Ah, Mr. Maxted," said Mr. Swift.

"I know you," said Leo. "You're the guy who asked about my 911 interface at the science fair."

Mr. Swift shook the man's hand and said, "Leo, this is Anton Maxted, chairman of the board of Futol Industries."

Leo said, "Glad to meet you. Futol?

Aren't they the people who provide computer services to the government?''

"State and local government services, Leo,'' said Maxted. He seated himself on the edge of the bed. "You know, I never did have the chance to see how your program works.''

Leo's eyes widened. "That's right! You had to leave before I . . . demonstrated it.''

Leo stole a quick glance at Tom and Rick, but both kept straight faces. Sandra had turned her back on the conversation, looking at something suddenly fascinating through the window.

"Well, Leo,'' Maxted said, "my company is quite interested in your, ah, invention. When you have fully recovered, we'd like you to come over and give us a personal demonstration.''

He reached into a vest pocket and removed a business card. "Here,'' he said, placing it by Leo's pillow. "Give me a call when you're out of the hospital.''

Leo was stunned. It was the last thing he had expected. "Gosh. I certainly will, Mr. Maxted. Thank you.''

"Well, then,'' said Maxted. "I wish you a speedy recovery. Will you walk me to the elevator?'' he said to Mr. Swift.

"Certainly, Anton," Mr. Swift responded with a big smile.

"So long, everyone," said Maxted.

Tom and Rick congratulated Leo. Sandra walked over to him, leaned down, and gave him a big kiss on the cheek.

"I can't believe all this is happening," Leo said.

Tom and Sandra winked at each other, and Leo saw it.

"Wait a minute," he said. "This didn't just all happen, did it? Something tells me that the Swifts had a lot to do with it." He gave Tom a hard look.

"Okay, Leo. So Dad noticed that Mr. Maxted was at the fair. They've known each other for many years. But it was Maxted who called Dad, not the other way around. He assumed that Dad would know about 'the tall, shy fellow with the exciting idea,' and he was right."

Leo smiled gratefully at Tom. "I still owe you and Sandra a million times over."

"No—make that five million," said Tom.

Sandra laughed and said, "You know, Leo, you have more friends than you thought you had. We were really worried about you."

"Aw, you shouldn't have worried about

me, Sandra," Leo said. "After all, I was protected by your fire suit."

"And it almost got you killed!" she said.

"No, that was me," said Tom. Before Sandra could protest, he continued. "And by the way, Leo and I gave your suit a field test worthy of Rick's favorite motto."

Sandra looked confused.

"Test to destruction," Rick said with a grin.

"It will take only some minor modifications—like adding your grounding mechanism and a communications link—and the fire suit can go into production," said Tom with more than a touch of pride in his sister's accomplishment.

"And what about the fire bike, Tom?" asked Rick.

"Fire bike?"

"Yes—what you insist on calling the jet cycle," Rick explained.

"Oh," said Tom. "What about it?"

"Well, do you think it's been fully tested?"

A suspicious look crossed Tom's face. "Why do you ask, Rick?"

"Because," said Sandra before Rick could speak, "he has some crazy idea about borrowing it for our date tonight."

"Why," said Tom, "I think that's a great

idea! Rick, it still needs some kinks worked out, but who better to work them out than you and Sandra?" He smiled at his sister, and added, "If he gets out of line, you can drop him from an appropriate height!"

Everyone laughed but Rick.

"Tom, you sure know how to hurt a guy," Rick said with a pained expression.

"No, that's *me*," said Sandra. Rick turned around just in time to get hit with a pillow full in the face. Before he could recover, she took him by the arm. "Come on, fly-boy, it's time to go."

As they were leaving, Tom grabbed Rick and said, "He'll be right behind you, Sandra."

She turned without stopping. "Fine. I'll get the elevator."

Rick sat down next to Tom. "What's up?"

Tom's face was serious again as he said, "Rick, please—take good care of her."

Rick looked offended. "Come on, Tom. You know I always take the best care of Sandra."

"Not Sandra!" Tom said with a grin. "I mean the fire bike!"

Tom's next adventure:

Tom is putting the finishing touches on an astounding new device—a Total Reality Generator. A powerful computer interfaces with the human mind, re-creating the true-to-life conditions of space flight. But an untested program has been inserted into the system, and it's about to propel Tom into an uncharted fantasy world from which he may never return!

The program is based on Galaxy Masters, a role-playing game at Tom's school. But as the images and icons touch his nerves and surge into his mind, the game turns frighteningly authentic. Suddenly, he is drawn into battle with the most powerfully sinister forces of the imagination—locked in a life-and-death struggle with the master of evil . . . the Dark Lord . . . in Tom Swift #10, *Mind Games*.

Together for the First Time!

The Hardys' sleuthing skills join with Tom Swift's inventive genius in a pulse-pounding new breed of adventure ...

A
HARDY BOYS
AND
TOM SWIFT
ULTRA THRILLER™

TIME BOMB

A twist in time ... A twisted mind ...
A terrifying twist of fate for Frank
and Joe and Tom!

A dream that has long fired the human imagination has become a reality: time travel. But as Tom Swift and the Hardy boys are about to discover, the dream can become a nightmare in the blink of an eye. An attack force of techno-thugs, under the command of the evil genius the Black Dragon, have seized control of a top-secret time-warp trigger!

Frank, Joe, and Tom leap into battle—shock troops in a war that stretches across the aeons to the edge of time. But whether chasing asteroids or dodging dinosaurs, they know they haven't a moment to lose. They must stop the Dragon before he carries out his final threat: turning the time machine into the ultimate doomsday device!

COMING IN AUGUST 1992